Brothers Till Death

Brothers Till Death

ROBERT EYNON

A Black Horse Western

ROBERT HALE · LONDON

© Robert Eynon 1999
First published in Great Britain 1999

ISBN 0 7090 6551 5

Robert Hale Limited
Clerkenwell House
Clerkenwell Green
London EC1R 0HT

Typeset in North Wales by
Derek Doyle & Associates, Mold, Flintshire
Printed and bound in Great Britain by
WBC Book Manufacturers Limited, Bridgend

Dedicated to
my family in the Rhondda

ONE

Billy Nash held his cards loosely in his hand and waited for the feller on his left to open the bidding. Although Billy looked every bit the gambler in his fawn velvet jacket and silver-grey waistcoat, tonight the play seemed lack-lustre and dull as the weather outside in the street, where the rain was falling steadily and forming puddles in the ruts left by the wheels of the carriages and wagons.

Billy's lethargy contrasted with the mood of his employer Mr Braithwaite. Braithwaite had been in a state of excitement ever since the stagecoach had drawn up outside his hotel a couple of hours earlier and deposited a certain Miss Mary Liddell into the saloonkeeper's safekeeping until the following morning when she would resume her journey towards the Texas border.

Billy hadn't seen the girl yet, but those who had quickly spread the story that she was the prettiest creature they'd come across in a month of Sundays. One of them even produced a picture of the girl that they'd cut out of a poster advertising a vaudeville show she'd appeared in the previous fall in St Louis.

'And if you think she looks pretty in this picture,' he told everyone within range, 'you wanna see her in real life. There ain't a prettier young filly in the whole state.'

Apart from her good looks it appeared that Miss Liddell could also sing a fair song and had already earned a considerable reputation as an entertainer back East. But as Billy Nash eyed his adversaries and joined in the bidding the girl was nowhere to be seen. No doubt she'd be dining in the seclusion of her room before retiring early to bed; the bumping and swaying of a stagecoach was a wearing experience, especially for a woman. Much as he'd like to get a glimpse of the young lady and see for himself if she really was as pretty as fellers claimed, Billy put her out of his mind and turned to the serious business of winning enough money to pay Mr Braithwaite the sort of commission that would keep him happy.

It was about nine-thirty that the piano came to

life suddenly, and simultaneously a buzz of excitement ran through the motley throng of drinkers and gamblers who filled the large room. Billy looked up from his cards and watched the girl make her way down the red-carpeted staircase. The saloonkeeper had obviously been waiting for this moment and had signalled to the pianist to provide a musical accompaniment to the young lady's descent.

In spite of the heavy, smoke-filled atmosphere Billy could see that Miss Mary Liddell was indeed beautiful. She wore a long blue dress that provided a soft background to the long blonde hair that fell halfway down her back. No doubt she would truss it up during a stage performance, but tonight she was relaxing after a long day on the road.

By the time she reached the foot of the stairs the room was strangely silent, apart from the tinkling of the piano keys, but one man was moving quickly to intercept the girl. That man was Braithwaite, the saloonkeeper, who was determined to do his darnedest to persuade Miss Liddell to sing at least one number and give his clients something to talk about for the rest of their lives.

Braithwaite engaged his guest in an earnest,

whispered conversation for a few moments before she smiled a smile that seemed to light the whole room and nodded her head in acquiescence. Cheeks flushed, the saloonkeeper turned and ushered the girl over to the piano; he had every reason to be pleased with himself, since he'd gone out on a limb. If the girl had refused his request he'd have been a laughing-stock in his own saloon and outside.

As Miss Liddell and the pianist engaged in a tête-à-tête to agree on items they were both familiar with, Braithwaite cleared his throat and addressed the hard-bitten audience and informed them that the famous songstress Miss Mary Liddell, who just happened to be the most illustrious guest to have honoured his humble hotel, had graciously consented to entertain them with a few songs from her repertoire. Of course, he added with a condescending glance in the direction of the pianist who was already sweating profusely from the responsibility which had been thrust upon him, Miss Liddell was accustomed to the accompaniment of a band of professional, er, polished musicians. However, he was sure that Lennie would do his best, and that their visitor's voice would shine through all adversity.

And shine it did. The girl thrilled the gathering

with a medley of sweet Irish numbers and finished off with a couple of old French ballads that couldn't fail to go down well here in Louisiana. When she'd done the applause was rapturous, and Lennie grinned broadly if toothlessly when the young star insisted that he rise from his chair and receive his fair share of the credit for his labours.

Meanwhile, Braithwaite had retired to the counter and was ordering a bottle of his finest champagne to reward Miss Liddell's graciousness. Hence he was not at hand to guide the girl back from the piano. As Mary Liddell hesitated as to what to do next now that the applause had died away, a tall, heavily built man lurched suddenly towards the piano and grabbed her unceremoniously by the arm.

From where he sat at the gaming-table Billy Nash saw the girl grimace with annoyance and pain as the feller's stubby fingers closed on her bare arm. The gambler knew the man by sight and reputation; Cab Barlow had blown into town a few days earlier, fortunately not accompanied by his two cousins, Josh and Dill, who were wanted killers in several states of the Union.

Cab was a rough, hard man in his own right and he maintained close ties with his hoodlum

11

relations, but thus far he'd never been identified as taking part in any of their most serious transgressions. However, he had a bullying side to his nature, and when he was confronted by anyone who'd stand up to him and likely as not beat him, he traded on the fear that folk felt towards Josh and Dill Barlow. He could always bum a free drink in a saloon just at the mention of his cousins' names, and his very size and mean disposition were enough to scare the more timid of his victims into submission.

Seeing that nobody else in the room would do more than mutter about Cab's oafish behaviour, Billy Nash nodded to a fellow hired gambler who was standing idly at the bar.

'Take over my hand,' he told the man. 'I'm quitting.'

He rose from his seat and made his way swiftly to the centre of the room, where the girl was struggling to break the big feller's hold. Despite his rather advanced years the pianist joined in on the singer's side but his only reward was to be thrown back noisily against the black and ivory keyboard. When Cab Barlow turned and saw the smartly dressed gambler confronting him, he leered drunkenly and confidently.

'Out of my way, dude,' he snarled. 'The little

lady wants to buy me a drink.'

Billy turned his head as if to talk to the girl and confirm what Cab had said, but without losing sight of the big man from the corner of his eye. Thinking he'd suckered the gambler, Cab threw a roundhouse right hand at the smaller man's head.

It would have been easy for Billy to slip under the punch and let his opponent lose his balance, but in that event he'd have dragged the girl down with him, which would have been an undignified and humiliating spectacle for Miss Liddell to endure. So instead, the gambler held his ground and blocked the clumsy punch with his upraised left arm.

Both Cab's arms were committed now since he hadn't released his hold on the girl, but Billy Nash's right hand was still free so he dug it deep into the big man's midriff. The whole room heard the grunt as the air shot out through Cab Barlow's gaping mouth. At the same moment the girl felt the steely grip relax on her arm and she pulled herself free and backed against the side of the piano.

The gambler glimpsed the ugly red marks on the young lady's pale skin and his eyes narrowed into slits. Mary Liddell had done nothing to deserve such treatment. Billy followed his initial jab with a jarring right hand that landed on the base of the big man's ribcage.

Although he was slight of build the gambler was lithe and strong and when the second punch reached its target Cab Barlow emitted a stifled scream of pain. Then the bully's sluggish brain reacted at last and he dropped both hands in an attempt to save his tortured body regions from further punishment.

That too was a mistake; quick as a flash Billy switched his attack to the head. His left hand snaked upwards and opened a cut above his opponent's eye, and then he put a rapid end to the entertainment with a vicious right cross that almost lifted Cab Barlow's head from his shoulders. The big man's eyes rolled and his legs shook like jelly before he keeled over onto the floor and lay there unmoving.

You could have heard a pin drop in the crowded hall. Billy looked solicitously across at the girl to make sure that she was all right. Her smile reassured him and filled him with a warm feeling inside. She'd recovered her composure rapidly now that the danger was past.

'I'd like to buy you a drink, mister,' she told him. 'I reckon you deserve one; and maybe I do, too.'

Billy nodded his head mutely. The girl was so

pretty he was completely tongue-tied. But one thing he did know; she didn't need to do anything more to thank him. That smile had been enough.

TWO

Braithwaite the saloonkeeper had prepared a small table for two to entertain his guest and the bottle of champagne was standing in an ice bucket waiting to be uncorked. He was more than somewhat put out when Miss Liddell acknowledged his invitation to join him, yet insisted upon bringing the hired gambler along in her wake.

'Champagne!' the girl exclaimed as Braithwaite held the chair for her to sit down. 'For us?'

Braithwaite gave a little cough and muttered something about wishing to thank her for the wonderful performance she'd just given. He played with the idea of apologizing to her for Cab Barlow's behaviour but decided that the incident was best forgotten. The singer had other ideas.

'I thought our friend here gave a much more impressive performance than me,' she said, smiling sweetly at the gambler. 'By the way,' she added, 'I don't even know your name.'

'Billy. Billy Nash.'

The young lady eyed the two glasses standing on the table.

'You'll need more glasses, Mr Braithwaite,' she informed the saloon-owner.

He stared at her open-mouthed as she went on to explain.

'I take it that you will be taking a drink as well, Mr Braithwaite,' she said. 'And when you've popped the cork perhaps you'd be kind enough to take a glass over to my accompanist. Oh, and tell him while you're there that Miss Liddell really enjoyed working with him.'

She turned to the gambler, who was still standing there awkwardly.

'Please sit down, Billy,' the girl said. 'You're in Mr Braithwaite's way.'

The saloonkeeper's face was a picture as he hesitated and then reluctantly carried out the girl's wishes. Meanwhile the pianist had struck up a honky-tonk melody to celebrate the departure of Cab Barlow who was being carried through the swing-doors by four hefty customers.

'It's for you, Lennie,' Braithwaite said, slamming the glass down on the piano-top, and the

17

piano-player looked up in surprise. 'It wasn't my idea,' the saloon-owner informed him coldly. 'You can thank Miss Mary Liddell.'

He decided against rejoining the singer and the hired gambler. They were engaged in deep conversation. What the heck, Braithwaite thought, I don't like champagne anyways; and he went and consoled himself with a bottle of bourbon and the company of his usual cronies from the town's business community.

Back at the table Mary Liddell was studying her companion's slim, handsome features as if she was trying to read his mind.

'I was pretty scared back there,' she said. 'I hope it didn't show.'

Her frank gaze bothered and confused him. Was she referring to the impromptu singing or to the tussle with Cab Barlow? He took a swig of his champagne and coughed when the bubbles hit his throat. It tasted just like cider to his unrefined palate, though it was not as flat. All in all he'd have preferred a cold beer.

'It didn't show,' he assured her. 'Besides, moving about like you do I guess you get used to unexpected situations.'

'I can see that you're used to handling trouble, Billy,' she complimented him. 'Apart from the pianist nobody else dared lend a hand.'

'That's because the big feller has a reputation,' Billy said.

'But that didn't worry you.'

'Nope,' he agreed with a shy smile. 'Reputations never killed nobody.'

Despite the way he dressed, Billy Nash didn't really convince her as a professional gambler. He looked naturally athletic and muscular and his face lacked the pallor she usually associated with men who lived, and sometimes died, at the gaming-tables.

'You haven't always worked in saloons, have you?' she remarked.

'Nope,' he replied. 'I earn my living any way I can. Gambling's one of the easiest ways I know, provided you keep away from the booze; but I'm always ready to learn new trades.'

She watched him over the rim of her glass. Her eyes were of a deep, intense blue.

'What about you?' he asked suddenly. 'You seem mighty young to be so well travelled.' She looked no more than twenty to him.

She smiled to acknowledge the compliment but didn't answer for a few moments.

'I've performed on the stage since the time I could walk,' she told him. 'Or at least as far back

19

as I can remember. My parents are from Virginia and they have music and dancing in their blood. The Liddells have always been entertainers, and entertainers have to keep on the move. I've never known any other kind of life.'

He made a show of glancing around the room.

'Where are those parents of yours?' he enquired rhetorically. 'I don't see them.'

The girl laughed and the sound was soft and lovely like her singing. 'You know what happens to fledglings,' she said. 'Eventually they have to spread their wings and leave the nest.'

'And eventually build a nest of their own,' Billy suggested and the girl's eyes sparkled.

'Maybe,' she replied. 'At least, I hope so.'

'Any place in particular?' the gambler enquired. 'To build that nest, I mean.'

'Texas,' Mary Liddell informed him. 'You see, I met a most wonderful man when I was singing in St Louis.'

Billy's heart sank at the news. He'd only known her a few minutes yet already she felt a part of his life.

Fortunately, she didn't notice any change in him so she went on blithely, 'He's a banker,' she explained. 'He was in St Louis on business. After he saw me sing he kept sending me the most wonderful bouquets of flowers every night. At first my folks disapproved, but when he called to see them even my father was impressed. He . . . he's just so distinguished.'

'Your father?' Billy joked to lighten the conversation. He'd taken a dislike to the banker already.

'No,' the girl laughed. 'Wilbur.'

The gambler was thinking quickly. 'Distinguished' seemed an odd way to describe the man she might end up marrying.

'He ain't young then,' he commented, and the girl inclined her head to one side.

'He's neither young nor old,' she said. 'He hasn't told me his age but I reckon he's about forty. And I'd say that you're in your late twenties, Billy.'

'Twenty-eight,' he informed her. 'By the way, where in Texas does he hail from?'

'Oh, he isn't a Texan,' the singer replied. 'He's from New York, but after the war he decided to move out West. Eventually he found himself in a township called Cedar Hollow. It's a small place, he tells me, but it's growing and has plenty of potential what with the settlers and the open spaces for cattle.'

This time she did notice the reaction in Billy Nash's face. The gambler's expression had clouded over.

21

'D'you know Cedar Hollow?' she inquired.

'I oughta,' Billy replied. 'I was born on a homestead less than ten miles from the town.'

'Maybe you know my fiancé then,' she said eagerly before correcting herself. 'Well our engagement hasn't been made formal yet. His full name is Wilbur Hawkins.'

She looked disappointed when Billy shook his head.

'I don't know him,' he told her. 'I ain't been home since the war.'

She looked at him in surprise; the civil war had been over for five years. But he was avoiding her gaze now as if he didn't want to answer any more questions. She raised the near-empty bottle and poured the last of the champagne into his glass.

'I'll have to go up to my room soon,' she said. 'All this excitement has taken it out of me, and I don't want to miss the stage tomorrow.'

She reached across and tapped his hand affectionately.

'It's been nice knowing you, Billy,' she said. 'I hope we'll meet again some day.'

She sounded as if she meant it.

THREE

After the pleasant interlude in the company of Miss Mary Liddell the gaming-tables held little appeal for Billy Nash. Seeing that the replacement dealer had settled in comfortably and that Braithwaite the saloonkeeper was safely ensconced among his drinking buddies, the gambler ambled over to the counter and ordered a beer.

Billy was not normally much of a drinker since his work demanded sharp wits and self-discipline. Tonight, however, he was feeling very relaxed as if the young lady's presence had remained with him even after she'd said goodnight and gone upstairs. In addition, several of the saloon clientele were eager to congratulate him on the fight and insisted on buying him a drink to celebrate his victory over his loutish opponent.

He must have drunk at least half-a-dozen beers to add to the champagne he'd shared with Mary

Liddell. The lights in the hall were beginning to dance a little before his eyes when he finally managed to tear himself away from his admirers and make his way to the swing-doors leading to the street. Outside the heavy rain had desisted but a curtain of fine spray was still descending. Despite the dampness Billy felt happy, like a man in love.

The alcohol in his veins and the slippery surface of the sidewalk made for slow progress as he headed for his lodgings. He'd gone maybe a hundred yards when he heard the first shot. Further along the street somebody shouted a warning and passers-by began to run for cover. Fuddled as he was, the gambler didn't react until a second shot tore a sizeable chunk out of a wooden porch just a few feet from his head.

Billy had no idea where the shooting was coming from, but he was certain of the target – himself! There was only one thing he could do, run. He dropped into a crouch and made for the nearest side-street which offered him welcome darkness for concealment. When he reached it he felt safer already. Only a fool would pursue him into the shadows from the relative brightness of the main thoroughfare.

Billy assessed his situation: he could draw his

gun and venture back on to the main street, but still not knowing where his enemy was located; he could make his way back to his lodgings via the back-streets, but only to spend a sleepless night wondering if his attacker had traced him there; or thirdly, he could hang around in the darkness and bide his time until he came face to face with Cab Barlow, since he was by now convinced of the sniper's identity.

He chose the last option. His dander was up, but at least the shooting had cleared his head, and his mind was working logically. Cab Barlow was unlikely to go near the saloon from where he'd recently been ejected. He wasn't likely to enlist any support there. No, Cab was more likely to follow the route Billy himself had been taking before he'd been thrown off track by the gunshots.

Billy was fairly well acquainted with the side-streets of the town and he stuck to them for the next five minutes or so. He re-emerged at the corner of the main thoroughfare at one of its least well-lit parts, where the hotels and saloons petered out and gave way to two rows of shops that had closed hours before.

He remained motionless in the shadows and waited. Further along the street from whence he'd come men were still yelling out warnings that there was a madman at large. Then Billy saw a match flare suddenly in an alleyway across the street from where he stood.

Of course, it could have been anyone lurking there in the darkness, but Cab Barlow was a distinct possibility, since he was stupid enough, or maybe concussed enough, to light a smoke without thinking. A few moments went by and then the glow of the cigarette vanished suddenly. Billy guessed that the feller had turned his head and was moving deeper into the alleyway.

Glancing swiftly to left and right, the gambler strode across the road, pausing at the street corner to draw his Colt .45. There was still no sign of the cigarette glow. Flattening himself against the side of the building he edged his way into the darkness. When he'd advanced a few yards he called out softly, 'Cab . . . Cab Barlow.'

The cigarette glow reappeared as the man's head swung around. Billy could have opened fire there and then but he was unwilling to injure an innocent man. As he watched the cigarette was thrown to the ground and extinguished in the mud. Still there was no reply.

'Don't go any further, Cab,' Billy advised.

'They're waiting for you at the far end. You've got them all stirred up.'

'Who are you?' a voice asked.

'Just a friend,' the gambler replied, noting mentally that the man hadn't denied that he was Cab Barlow.

He sidled a couple of feet towards the sound of the voice, then a gun barked and a slug crashed into the woodwork in the spot he'd just vacated. The flash of the explosion betrayed the concealed gunman's location and Billy Nash thumbed the hammer of his Colt twice in rapid succession. He heard a grunt and a low moan, so he fired a third time for luck and was relieved to hear a thud as the man sprawled forwards on to the sodden earth.

Cautiously the gambler went and crouched over the body. There was no sign of movement or breathing. Sheathing his Colt he backed away and made for the street again. This time there really were folk waiting there. Two of them were sporting silver badges on their shirts and they had their guns drawn and levelled at his chest.

As soon as Billy was disarmed the small crowd became bolder and the usual wild accusations began to be bandied about.

'That's the feller, Marshal,' a man with a bad squint in his eye pronounced confidently. 'Fired a good half-dozen shots at us, then he ran off down this alleyway.'

Two drunks standing next to old squint-eye agreed heartily with his reading of the situation. Fortunately for the gambler there were others present who saw things differently.

'I was right next to this young feller when the shots was fired,' an old-timer chimed in. 'I was taking the air 'cos the rain had almost stopped. I saw him coming along the sidewalk towards me and he looked like he'd had a drink or two. Anyways the shot went pretty close to us; too darned close if you ask me, like as if it was meant for one of us. Anyways, I wasn't going to hang around long enough to find out.'

The town marshal was of medium height and slight build but sinewy. He was in his early forties; while his deputy, whom he'd already dispatched into the alleyway to take a look, was only in his twenties, if that. When the younger lawman returned he could hardly contain his excitement.

'That's Cab Barlow lying there,' he told the marshal. 'He's stone-dead. Jeez, Slim, we ain't heard the last of this!'

The marshal chewed thoughtfully on a twist of

tobacco and spat the juice on to the damp side-walk.

'We'd better get this feller over to the jailhouse,' he told his deputy. 'We gotta get things sorted out.'

A public-spirited bystander pushed his way through the crowd.

'Someone'll have to tell the undertaker before he's had too much to drink, Marshal,' he said. 'D'you want me to go?'

A few men laughed at the remark, but the lawman remained serious. 'Yeah, thanks,' he told the man. 'Tell him I'll make sure he gets paid for his trouble.'

The marshal and his deputy walked on either side of the gambler as they made their way over to the small stone jailhouse that was one of the oldest buildings in the town. It transpired that the two lawmen were close relatives, the marshal being his deputy's uncle.

'Lock the door, Hank,' he told his nephew. 'I don't want anyone barging in on us.'

The younger man did as he was told, then took up a position at one of the windows so that he could survey the length of the street. Meanwhile, his uncle sank wearily into a leather armchair behind the oak desk at the far end of the room. He motioned his visitor, guest or prisoner – Billy

Nash couldn't figure out quite what his status was – to sit down on an upright wooden chair opposite him.

The gambler complied, but didn't take his eyes off the lawman's face for a moment. He could tell that the older man's weariness was feigned and that his mind was sharp and fully equipped to get to the heart of the matter.

'I'm Slim Forbes,' the marshal said. 'I been town marshal for nearly ten years. Who are you?'

'Billy Nash,' the gambler replied.

'He's a card-sharp, Slim,' his nephew chimed in. 'I seen—'

'Shut your mouth, Hank,' the marshal said sharply. 'And keep your eyes on the street.'

Far from being annoyed, the youngster grinned and shrugged his shoulders. Billy could sense the bond of friendship between the two men despite the older man's irritation.

'I deal cards at the Lady Luck Hotel,' Billy said. 'The owner, Braithwaite, can vouch for me.'

'That'd help,' Forbes said. 'Hank?'

'Yeah?'

'Go tell Braithwaite we got his dealer in the jailhouse. Maybe he'll want to come over here.'

'Sure thing, Slim,' the youngster replied and went out into the street whistling happily. Billy wondered if this was the first killing the deputy had ever been involved in. His uncle turned back to the gambler.

'You'd better tell me how it happened,' he suggested, then added with a touch of irony, 'seeing that you seem to be the only surviving witness.'

Billy Nash did just that, starting off with the fistfight in the Lady Luck saloon bar, then moving on to the events in the street. His account was simple and factual, without embellishment. By the time he'd finished speaking the lawman had already reached a conclusion.

'Looks like he was holding a grudge against you after you'd stuck up for the young lady singer,' he said. 'He tried to bushwhack you, only you were too good for him.'

'I was lucky,' the gambler remarked, recalling the shot which had just missed his head.

'Either way, it don't add up to murder,' the lawman said. 'In my book you were just defending yourself.'

Billy felt a sense of relief flooding over him, but the marshal hadn't finished speaking.

'Cab Barlow was a violent man,' he pointed out, 'but his two cousins, Josh and Dill, are violent, mean and dangerous.'

'I got no quarrel with them,' the gambler said. 'I don't even know them.'

'That ain't how they're gonna see it,' Slim Forbes warned. 'Not once they hear Cab is dead. If I was you, I'd saddle up and find somewhere safer to live.'

Billy smiled at him.

'I ain't a quitter, Marshal,' he replied, 'and I ain't even got a horse. I was planning to stay a while longer. I like the place and I got a job here.'

Forbes shrugged his shoulders.

'There's a stage heading west tomorrow,' he said. 'Your singer friend will be on it. I reckon you should ride with her.'

The jailhouse door opened and the young deputy came in, his black hair glistening from the rain.

'Braithwaite won't come,' he informed his uncle. 'He says he don't want no trouble with any of the Barlows. As far as he's concerned this feller here don't work for him no more.'

The marshal glanced at the gambler to see how he'd taken the news. The smile had left Billy Nash's face and had been replaced by a thoughtful expression. Suddenly the morning stage out of town didn't seem such a bad idea after all.

FOUR

A week later an impatient Josh Barlow was waiting with his younger brother Dill for their cousin to show up at the rendezvous in Little Creek, a few miles east of the township of Oakhill where, unknown to them, Cab Barlow had met his death at the hands of Billy Nash.

Josh was tall and angular, with a thick moustache and a stubbly beard. His brother Dill was shorter and rather fleshier; Dill fancied himself as a ladies' man and usually made the effort to shave every day, even when they were on the run somewhere in the wilderness. Josh had won considerable renown for himself in face-to-face gun duels and he was sought after by men who were intent on building empires, or protecting the empires they'd already carved out for themselves. Dill was content to live in his elder brother's shadow; he avoided individual confrontations and preferred to fight in a gang with the odds on his side, or to shoot a man down from a concealed position.

'Where d'you reckon he's got to, Josh?' Dill asked for maybe the tenth time that afternoon. 'D'you reckon he's been hitting the bottle again?'

His brother looked at the horizon; the sun was low in the sky, yet cousin Cab had promised to meet them before noon.

'We gonna wait here till nightfall?' Dill inquired.

Josh Barlow shook his head.

'Nope,' he said. 'I'm going into town to find him.'

For a moment the younger man's hopes rose. Town meant saloons and saloons meant booze and women.

'I'll come with you, Josh,' he suggested hopefully.

'You'll stay right here,' Josh retorted. 'In case Cab shows up.'

Dill's spirits fell but he concealed his disappointment. Brother Josh wasn't in the best of moods.

'Well, you be careful, Josh,' he said. 'Someone's bound to recognize you.'

'The marshal in Oakhill is an old hand,' his brother replied. 'He ain't lived as long as he has

34

by going up against fellers like me. If I can get Cab out of there without him trying to tear the town apart, Slim Forbes ain't gonna stand in our way. If I ain't back in two hours, then you can start worrying.'

Braithwaite and several of his customers had quite a shock when Josh Barlow came through the swing-doors of the Lady Luck saloon bar as if he owned the place. Braithwaite was sitting alone in a gloomy corner of the room and he tried to make himself as small and inconspicuous as possible as the gunslinger's gaze swept around the assembled drinkers.

Actually Braithwaite and Josh Barlow were old friends and had even co-operated in some dubious enterprises when they were younger. Now, however, the saloonkeeper was a legitimate businessman and doing nicely for himself, so naturally he didn't relish the opportunity to renew his acquaintance-ship with a man whose reputation had gone from bad to worse in the intervening years.

Josh Barlow had other ideas. As soon as he spotted his old pardner he strode over to his table.

'Braithwaite,' he exclaimed with a smile that revealed several missing teeth. 'You and me got to talk somewhere private.'

Reluctantly, the saloonkeeper got to his feet and led his visitor into a small office under the staircase. Inside, Josh Barlow didn't beat about the bush.

'I'm looking for Cab,' he informed his reluctant host. 'You remember Cab, don't you? He was riding with us when we hit that bank in Jackson way back.'

Braithwaite remembered. He still bore a scar across his ribs to remind him every time he looked in a mirror. He decided to come clean with his unwelcome visitor in the hope that Josh would realize there was no point in hanging around long in Oakhill.

'Sure I remember him, Josh,' he replied. 'Only I'm afraid I got bad news for you – very bad news.'

'Bad news?'

'Yeah,' the saloonkeeper sighed hypocritically since he'd never liked Cab Barlow. 'Cab got himself killed in an alleyway across the street a week ago this very night.'

The gunslinger sat down heavily in a chair. The past few years had taken a heavy toll on the family. Now only he and Dill were left.

'You'd better tell me how it happened,' he said.

Braithwaite thought it wiser to omit any mention of the fight in his saloon bar which had sparked off the trouble. Instead, he concentrated on the action in the street and how Cab Barlow had died heroically, gunned down by a gambler named Billy Nash.

'This Billy Nash,' Josh Barlow asked sharply. 'Does he ever use this saloon?'

Braithwaite nervously swallowed some spittle that had formed in his throat.

'He used to,' he admitted. 'In fact he worked here for a while; but as soon as I heard that the marshal had him over in the jailhouse for killing Cab I sent word that he wasn't to set foot in the Lady Luck ever again.'

Fortunately, Josh Barlow didn't seem interested in the gambler's connections with the saloon.

'Is that where he is now, the jailhouse?' he asked.

'Nope; the marshal didn't keep him locked up. He just told him to be out of town by noon the next day. The gambler took the next stage heading west. There was a girl on the same stage. She was heading for a place called Cedar Hollow, Texas. You heard of it?'

Barlow shook his head but made a mental note of the name. When he stood up his face was still tense and drawn.

'I'll be back,' he informed the saloonkeeper. 'But first I got to settle accounts with this Nash feller. The marshal should have strung the sonofabitch up, only us Barlows only count when it's us who's doing the killing. Well, I got a long memory; I'll catch up with Slim Forbes later.'

As it turned out, he didn't have all that long to wait. As he left the saloon and made for the tethering-rail where he'd left his horse, the town marshal was waiting in the street to arrest him. At first Josh couldn't believe that the lawman would pull a gun on him like that, but a prod in the back from deputy Hank Forbes' rifle convinced him that the town's peacekeepers were not playing games.

On the way over to the jailhouse Slim casually inquired how their captive's brother Dill was making out.

'He's dead, Marshal,' the gunslinger lied smoothly. 'That's what I came to see Cab about. Him and Dill was always pretty close.'

'And even closer now, I guess,' Hank Forbes observed cheerfully and Slim allowed himself a wry smile at the thought of the Barlows' rapid decline.

Josh Barlow lay in the darkness of the cell and fought against dozing off. He guessed it was way past midnight by now and the young deputy marshal had been snoring for a few hours in his uncle's leather armchair.

Earlier in the evening Josh had listened to the two lawmen discussing his fate in a matter-of-fact tone before Marshal Slim Forbes had retired to the comfort of his own bed on the far side of town. They intended to keep their prisoner locked up in Oakhill until the county sheriff decided where and when he'd be brought for trial. In any event, they'd concluded, Josh was not long for this world and then the scourge of the Barlows would be a detail of history.

The outlaw kept sleep at bay by nursing his hatred of the two lawmen. They'd allowed a gambler to gun down one of his family and then leave town scot-free. Yet here Josh was, languishing in jail, though he'd never committed a crime within twenty miles of Oakhill.

A scraping sound above his head made him sit up suddenly on his bunk. Someone was rubbing metal across the bars of the window. Josh threw the grimy blanket to one side and rose stealthily to his feet. He pressed his face against the iron grid and made out his brother's features in the gloom. Dill had not let him down.

'Josh?' Dill's voice was a whisper, but to the

prisoner it seemed to resound like thunder.

'Sh . . .' he urged and his brother's voice fell even lower.

'I cain't get a gun to you, Josh,' he said. 'The bars are so close you cain't even squeeze a derringer through them.'

Hank Forbes stirred in the armchair; his left leg slipped suddenly off the wooden chair it had been resting on and crashed on to the stone floor. He blinked blearily in the weak light of the oil-lamp and then he tuned in to the sound that had disturbed his slumbers. Groaning and retching noises were coming from the prisoner's cell.

'Shut up, Josh,' he called out irritably. 'You're gonna wake them fellers on Boothill!'

The noises didn't abate, so Hank got up wearily and ambled over to the cell door. The capture of a wanted outlaw like Josh Barlow was one thing, since it could only enhance the reputation of an up-and-coming young deputy like himself; however, if Josh choked to death in captivity there'd be a suspicion of foul play that would do him and his uncle Slim no good at all.

Of course, it might all be a bluff; but that didn't worry him none since he was the one holding the six-shooter in his hand. He unlocked the cell door and then went back for the oil-lamp. All the time he kept the Colt pointed at the figure writhing under the blanket.

'Let's have a look at you, Josh,' he said as he neared the bunk. 'D'you need water?'

As he raised the lamp higher for light he caught a glimpse of the gun-barrel jutting through the bars of the window. He had no time to react; Dill Barlow pressed the trigger and sent a slug smashing into the deputy marshal's temple from less than five feet. Blood and brains rained down over the blanket but Josh Barlow didn't care about that. He was on his feet in an instant, groping for the dead man's gun.

'Get the horses round to the front,' he ordered his brother. 'Let's get out of here pronto!'

FIVE

Although Billy Nash didn't much like leaving Oakhill under the present circumstances, the company of Miss Mary Liddell proved ample compensation for his loss. The gambler reckoned that it was fate that was taking him back to the home he hadn't seen since the early days of the war.

As he relaxed into the swaying movement of the coach that carried them westwards his mind was divided between present realities and memories of his childhood and adolescence before the strife which had made a man of him, and a corpse of many of his friends.

'We were three brothers,' he told his travelling companion. 'James, who was the eldest, me, and the youngest, Tyrone, or Ty as we used to call him.'

42

'What about your parents?' Mary Liddell asked. 'Are they still alive?'

A cloud passed over Billy's face.

'They were alive when James and me left for the army,' he said. 'Only, my pa wasn't in good health. That's why the army didn't take Ty; they let him stay on and run the homestead.'

He stared out of the window at the distant hills as if his family's history was written on them.

'I was at Fredericksburg one December when I heard that the winter had been too hard for Pa to take. It was my mother who wrote the letter to tell me. A few months later it was Ty's turn to write: Ma had gone down with a fever all of a sudden and the doc had arrived too late to save her.'

'Did the army give you leave to pay your respects?' Mary Liddell enquired gently.

'I didn't want to,' Billy replied almost fiercely. 'I just blamed the North for starting the war in the first place. I set about killing as many darned Yankees as I could get in my sights.' He paused for a moment. 'My brother James survived until the last few months of the war. He was wounded at Columbia, Carolina and gangrene set in. They amputated his leg but the shock killed him. Our troops were in full retreat at the time; most of the wounded weren't even given treatment.'

'But your brother Tyrone,' the girl prompted him. 'Did he survive the war?'

'Yeah, he survived,' Billy said quietly. 'Only, I ain't ever been back to see him.'

'You don't get on with him?' the young singer enquired.

'Sure I get on with him,' the gambler replied. 'The three of us all got on together, except when we were fighting amongst ourselves like brothers always do from time to time.'

'Well, why didn't you go back?' Mary Liddell persisted.

Billy rubbed the side of his face.

'I guess I was really down when we lost the war after so much fighting against the odds. I couldn't face meeting the folk who'd put their faith in us and explaining to them what had gone wrong. Besides, my own folk were dead and everything would have been different. I thought I'd wait a few months before I went back; and then the months turned into years.'

'Tell me what he's like,' Mary said. 'Ty, I mean.'

Billy smiled as he pondered the question. He was talking to Mary Liddell as he hadn't talked to anyone in years.

'Ty's a year younger than me,' he said. 'But he's probably taller than me by now. Last time I saw

44

him he was catching up fast.'

'And you both liked fighting,' Mary remarked with a twinkle in her eyes.

'We all did,' Billy laughed. 'We fought the kids from the other homesteads, but mostly we joined forces with them against the boys from Cedar Hollow. Ma used to make us go to school there, and to church on Sundays. We were known as the fighting Nashes, and we made up a motto of our own: "Brothers Till Death". James was two years older than me, so he always led the charge. Ty was a devil, though; he'd take on boys of James' age and beat them. I could handle a gun better than either of them, but in a fistfight James always ended up beating me because he was bigger, and Ty could always bloody my nose because he was kinda lean and rangy.'

Mary Liddell shook her head in mock disapproval.

'I hope your brother Ty hasn't landed himself in any serious trouble since you've been gone,' she said. 'He sounds like someone who might need an elder brother to give him advice from time to time.'

'Not Ty,' the gambler corrected her. 'In the last letter I got from him at the end of the war he told me he was courting the pastor's daughter, Janie

Jones. He didn't sound like the old Ty at all; he even said he might think about becoming a pastor himself some day!'

The parting of their ways came all too soon for Billy Nash despite the fact that they'd journeyed together with only the occasional additional passenger for three days. Familiar clusters of trees and patterns of rocks and ridges told the gambler that he was nearing his home. With a mixed feeling of relief and regret he poked his head out of the window and called on the stage-driver to slow down.

'The farm's over the brow of that hill,' he explained to the girl. 'I can walk it from here in under an hour.'

He had only one small bag to hold all his possessions. As he stood alone on the dusty trail he looked rather lost.

'Don't forget to come to Cedar Hollow and look me up,' the young singer reminded him. 'Just ask for Wilbur Hawkins. Folk there may not know me, but they'll all have heard of Wilbur.'

Her voice had a note of pride that saddened him and made him feel almost an outsider in his own land. The stage pulled away but still the girl waved to him. Then she raised her handkerchief to her eye as if a tear had formed.

The sun was hot on his back and soon he'd divested himself of his jacket and was carrying it over his arm. Despite the sweat running down his face, it felt good to be back in familiar surroundings, though he was still apprehensive about meeting Ty again after so many years. He was afraid that the homestead would be no more than an empty shell now that his parents and elder brother were dead.

When he reached his destination things were even worse than he'd imagined them. There was no livestock to be seen and the front door of the house was wide-open and about to fall off its hinges. He'd imagined that his brother would still be working the smallholding but that was a mistake.

He entered the house and saw the familiar furniture now covered in a deep layer of dust. He went into the bedroom he'd shared with his two brothers. James' single bed was still there, and so was the double-bunk where he and Ty had slept. He could almost hear the laughter as he recalled the games they'd played in the darkness until their ma or pa had come into the room and sternly called them to order.

47

He glanced out of the window at the slope leading up to the woods. His heart missed a beat as he spotted the two wooden crosses less than a hundred yards from the house. It hadn't occurred to him that his parents would be buried on the homestead rather than on Cedar Hollow's Boothill. He went out of the house and walked up to the twin mounds of earth with a sense of awe. Although both crosses were badly weathered, his ma and pa's names were still clearly visible.

He stood there in silence for a few minutes, savouring his memories, when he was brought back to the present by the sound of horse's hooves.

He turned his head and watched the lone rider approach from the direction of the stage trail. He didn't much like what he saw; the rider was clean-shaven with an arrogant expression born of belief in his own abilities.

Before Billy had time to greet the stranger, the man had fired a question at him.

'What the hell d'you think you're doing on this land?'

'Just paying my respects to my folks,' the gambler replied calmly.

The rider glanced dismissively at the graves.

'This is Ty Nash's old place,' he said.

'That's right,' Billy agreed, glad to be speaking

48

to an acquaintance of his brother. 'Ty's my younger brother.'

'Ty did have an elder brother,' the rider snapped. 'Only he was killed by the Yankees. Ty's told me the story often enough when he's drunk – which is most of the time.'

Billy could feel his cheeks flush; like his brothers his temper was legendary in these parts, though the rider seemed unaware, or unconcerned, at the effect his words were having.

'I'm his other brother,' the gambler said icily. 'Name's Billy.'

The horseman tugged at his jacket to reveal a pearl-handled Colt in its holster.

'You're lying, mister,' he snarled. 'Ty ain't got no brother.'

Billy felt suddenly relaxed, as he always did when he knew that trouble was unavoidable.

'You talk real big,' he told the rider. 'Can you back it up?'

'I can back it up,' the man assured him, dropping his hand on to his gun.

He was wrong. His Colt was barely clear of the holster when Billy's shot lifted him clean out of the saddle and sent him crashing to the ground.

Billy Nash stood over the inert body and wiped the sweat from his brow. What had happened was crazy; he hadn't come here to kill a man, but he'd had no choice. He sat down at the side of his mother's grave and wondered what to do next.

SIX

Wilbur Hawkins stood at the window of his office and stared moodily out on to the main street of Cedar Hollow. The banker wasn't in the best of tempers despite the fact that his fiancée, Mary Liddell, had arrived on the stagecoach the previous evening as she'd promised.

Hawkins was a pale, angular man whose jet-black hair had turned grey in the region of his sideburns and whose forehead was heavily lined by years of concentration and scheming. He attributed his lack of joy at seeing Mary again to the complexities of his business dealings; for five long years he'd worked to build up his commercial bank and he'd poked a finger into every financial venture of significance in the area. But the time was fast approaching when Hawkins intended to reap where he'd sown.

51

Generally speaking he'd been well received in this Texas township, even if he was a darned Yankee. The southern states were destitute after the ravages of war. Hawkins brought money with him, even if some bad tongues said it was stolen money, and he used that money to prop up Cedar Hollow's ailing economy.

But Wilbur Hawkins was not the philanthropist he made himself out to be; every loan, every favour, was accompanied by a complicated written contract of which the small print was always the most important element. Mary Liddell had arrived at the very moment that the banker had begun to scrutinize these contracts afresh. Many of the local citizenry had taken the bait when times were tough. Now was the time for him to start reeling in the line.

Such was his preoccupation with his plans that he was only able to spare his fiancée an hour of his time when she arrived at Cedar Hollow. He used it in a practical manner, to install her in Miss Nellie Duke's boarding-house just off the main street. If Mary Liddell had been anticipating a candle-lit meal she was disappointed. Hawkins had a prior engagement and she'd had to share a table with Miss Nellie and three other guests.

There was a tap on the office door and a small, dark woman of indeterminate age came into the room. Her hair was drawn back in a severe bun and her features bore no trace of make-up. Ann Forest was Hawkins' personal secretary and she lived for her master.

'Mr Jay is waiting outside,' she informed him. 'He has an appointment for ten o'clock. Do you need me to take notes?'

He shook his head and she looked disappointed. However, she hadn't finished.

'A Miss Liddell called in the bank and asked to see you,' she said. 'I told her it wasn't possible, that you were too busy.'

Her voice had a sharp edge to it that amused him. So Miss Forest had met Miss Liddell, he thought. What a contrast! He walked over to his desk and scribbled a brief note: *I'll call for you at midday.* He handed the note to his secretary without bothering to fold it.

'Get one of the boys to take it over to the boarding-house,' he told her. 'Then show Jay in.'

Jay owned a large timber-yard on the outskirts of town. When Hawkins had first come to Cedar Hollow the timber-yard resembled the rest of the township; it was run-down and dilapidated. The banker had gone in person to see Jay and point

53

out to him that an efficient timber-yard was essential for the future development of the area.

'What development?' Jay had enquired sarcastically. 'There ain't no money for development. Well, I sure ain't got none.'

Hawkins had worked on Jay for weeks, wining and dining him in the Blue Star saloon which had belonged to one of the town's original founders, but which was now owned by the banker lock, stock and barrel. Eventually Jay had been talked into accepting a substantial loan which allowed him to expand his business and give employment to some of the war veterans who'd drifted back to Cedar Hollow at the end of hostilities. At the same time Wilbur Hawkins was financing the building of new homes and stores so that soon everybody was feeling relatively prosperous and confident for the future.

Jay the timber-merchant felt particularly fortunate since Hawkins seemed unworried if repayments were not made bang on time. Jay had a wife and three daughters with expensive tastes in clothes and they always managed to spend money as fast, or faster, than Jay could make it. Still, as long as the banker was so understanding nobody really gave the matter much thought.

This morning, as the timber-merchant entered

Hawkins' office, he was his usual cheerful self. Within five minutes he was reduced to an ashen-faced, trembling wreck as the banker-turned-torturer stung him repeatedly with accusations of financial incompetence and moral cowardice.

'Your business is in a mess,' Hawkins told him. 'You've let yourself slide over eighteen thousand dollars in debt to the bank. You've let your family run wild; God only knows how much them women of yours owe here in Cedar Hollow, not to mention all those orders they keep getting from back East.'

'I . . . I never realized,' Jay mumbled. 'You never warned me about falling behind in my payments. And the timber-mill's going real well.'

Wilbur Hawkins greeted the words with a derisive snort.

'The timber-mill's running on air,' he sneered. 'And soon it's gonna come to earth with a crash. The bank cain't keep lending out money to see it thrown away on satin and lace. Other businesses need my help, so I've decided to call time on old, bad debts and use the money to finance men who want to make something of themselves, not has-beens like you, Jay.'

Jay's voice and expression were piteous as he pleaded for his survival.

'I need time, Wilbur,' he said. 'I gotta sort things

out, realize my assets.'

Assets? What assets? he thought bitterly to himself. Would the pawnbroker be interested in fine ladies' garments and expensive ornaments that fell apart merely if you looked at them too hard? He was so deep in thought that he hardly heard the banker's final warning.

'You've got one week, Jay,' Hawkins told him. 'Else you lose your property to the bank.'

When Wilbur Hawkins left the bank just before midday he was in much better spirits. Things were beginning to move. Next he needed to see Tomkinson, the attorney, to discuss the issue of the homesteads.

'Mr Hawkins.'

He turned his head and saw Marshal Nelmes approaching from the direction of the jailhouse.

'Yeah, Nelmes, what is it?'

The lawman removed his Stetson as a mark of respect.

'Potts ain't been seen since yesterday,' he said. 'His horse walked into town an hour ago, all saddled up but without a rider.'

Hawkins took out a gold watch from his waist-coat-pocket and studied it for a moment.

'If Potts got thrown from his horse, send the boys out to look for him,' he suggested.

'A carter spotted the horse this morning,' Nelmes said. 'It was a mile out of town and a feller was riding it; only it wasn't Potts.'

The banker stared at him.

'That don't make sense,' he said.

'Well, the carter knows Potts and he knows the horse. The rider wheeled away as soon as he spotted the cart. He was kinda duded up. The carter reckons he might recognize him again.'

'Good. Tell him to keep his eyes open. There'll be something in it for him if he's right. Can I leave it with you?'

'Sure thing, Mr Hawkins,' the lawman replied. 'I'll see to it.'

Tomkinson was putting the finishing touches to a legal contract when the banker strode into his office without knocking. The lawyer had changed since the early days of their acquaintanceship; he no longer bristled at Hawkins' arrogance. The bank threw enough business his way to provide a comfortable living for him and his beloved wife, Kathryn.

'I was just going to lunch,' Tomkinson said with an ingratiating smile. 'Would you care to join me?'

'Nope, I got company already,' the banker informed him. 'I need to see you this afternoon concerning the homestead association.'

The association in question consisted of a motley group of country hicks that Hawkins cultivated and pandered to for no apparent reason. The lawyer had much more important matters to attend to, but he hid his irritation and smiled at his visitor.

'Sure thing, Wilbur,' he said. 'Will two o'clock be early enough?'

As the banker walked out into the street he almost collided with a tall, attractive woman in her late thirties. Their eyes met and he could tell that she was angry with him. The news of his fiancée's arrival had travelled quickly.

'Hello, Kathryn,' Hawkins greeted her. 'Is Jeffrey taking you out to lunch?'

'That's right,' she said, almost in a hiss. 'And I hear you've got company as well.'

He met her gaze with equanimity. He and Mrs Tomkinson had been having a secret affair for over two years. Well, the way he saw it, if he could share her with her husband she could share him with his wife-to-be.

'That's right,' he confirmed, then added with a wink, 'but you know, Kathryn, I don't think my life is going to change all that much.'

She chewed the matter over and a slow smile replaced the pout on her lips. It amused him to see how easily women could be swayed from one emotion to another. His secretary, Ann Forest, was exactly the same; a harsh word from his lips could ruin her day, while his smile could make her heart miss a couple of beats.

'That's good,' Mrs Tomkinson said. 'When things are going so well, change can only make them worse.'

He'd chosen to eat at his own Blue Star saloon so that Mary Liddell could see how deferential everyone was towards him. The girl was already waiting for him at a table in a quiet recess.

'How is Miss Nellie treating you?' he enquired as he sat down opposite her.

'She's very nice,' Mary replied. 'In fact, the boarding-house is fine – for a short stay.'

He passed over the remark and invited her to choose a wine to accompany the meal.

'I didn't know you owned this place,' she said suddenly. 'The bartender told me.'

'This place and a few others,' Hawkins said modestly.

'Do you think I could sing here?' the girl asked. 'There doesn't seem to be much else for me to do in Cedar Hollow.'

The banker shook his head emphatically.

'There'll be lots for you to do, darling,' he

replied. 'Besides, it wouldn't do my image much good if folk thought you had to sing for a living.'

'But I like singing,' Mary said with a hint of stubbornness in her voice. 'It's because I'm a singer that we met, remember?'

The bartender arrived with the soup and cut the conversation short. As Wilbur Hawkins tucked his serviette under his collar it occurred to him that maybe all women were not the same after all.

SEVEN

The next morning Billy Nash knew he was taking a gamble in choosing to ride most of the way to Cedar Hollow on the dead man's horse. The alternative was a ten-mile hike carrying his belongings. When the wagon appeared suddenly on the horizon he realized the risk was too great for comfort, so he turned the horse to one side and galloped off into the sun. He later abandoned it in fresh pasture and made the remaining mile or so of the journey on foot.

Cedar Hollow looked more prosperous and extensive than he remembered it. Certainly there were people there he didn't remember from the old days. The place was quite bustling and nobody paid any attention to him as if nowadays they were used to strangers paying the township a visit.

The church was still a prominent landmark, with its bell-tower projecting above most of the other buildings. He decided to make it his first port of call, or rather the church-house which was home to Pastor Shad Jones, his wife Emma and their daughter Janie, who hopefully had maintained links with his brother Ty.

Emma Jones was just as he remembered her, though it took her a few moments to recognize the stranger standing on the doorstep. Once he'd confirmed his identity to her, she embraced him warmly and called out to the rest of the family.

'Shad, Janie, look who's here!'

The pastor's hair had greyed since their last meeting, and Janie had put on weight, which was a good thing because she'd been a scrawny youngster in her early teens when Ty, who was five years older than her, had first noticed she existed. Now she was in her early twenties and pretty, but with a certain sadness in her eyes that had maybe come with maturity. Before long the pastor's wife had a steaming coffee-pot on the oak table and Billy Nash was happily exchanging news with the family just like the old days.

'Sure the town has come on a lot since the war,' Shad agreed with the visitor's observation. 'It all began to happen when Wilbur Hawkins opened his bank on the main street. Not everybody likes Wilbur, what with him being a Yankee, but nobody can deny the effect he's had on Cedar Hollow.'

Billy glanced across at Emma Jones; judging by the expression on her face she didn't share her husband's enthusiasm for the banker.

'Well, I don't trust him,' Emma said in her usual blunt way. 'And I don't trust the men he's brought into town. They are gunfighters and they're not here to do us any good.'

The pastor smiled apologetically at their visitor.

'It's a sad fact that Texas is still a wild state,' he said. 'Wilbur has a lot of money invested in Cedar Hollow and he needs to protect it. Of course, we have a marshal. Do you remember Clem Nelmes, Billy?'

Billy thought for a moment and then nodded his head. He'd never been on very good terms with Clem, though that was in the old days when town and country youths had always fought one another as a matter of course.

'Well, Clem is officially the law in this town,' Shad explained. 'But Wilbur does employ a handful of men to protect his bank and other interests.'

Then Janie Jones spoke for the first time.

'Your brother Ty is Clem Nelmes' deputy,' she said. 'Though most of his time is spent cleaning up in Mr Hawkins' Blue Star saloon.'

Billy knew he had to be careful; although he'd buried the body deep in the woods the previous evening, a remark out of place in Cedar Hollow could easily incriminate him.

'I ain't had news of Ty since the war ended,' he said. 'How's he getting on?'

'Your brother's been a disappointment to us, Billy,' Shad Jones replied with a sigh. 'After he got the letter informing him of James' death he kinda went to pieces. I guess if you'd come home after the war like he was expecting, things might have been different. Luckily, Wilbur Hawkins has been good to him and kept him in work of sorts.'

Emma noticed the expression of guilt on Billy's face, and she decided to put the record straight.

'You can't put any blame on Billy,' she protested. 'Ty's no different from anybody else. We all suffered during the war. And what about the young fellers who came home maimed and blinded? Did Ty go through what they did? And don't tell me he's got any reason to thank Wilbur Hawkins. That man encouraged him to drink, or at least did nothing to stop him. Hawkins was looking for a local man who'd sort out any trouble that wasn't worth the attention of his gunslingers. Ty is still good with his fists, unfortunately, though sometimes I think more folk would stand up to him if he wasn't backed up by Wilbur's cronies.'

When it was time for their visitor to leave Shad Jones recommended the Mexican Trail saloon as a place for Billy to lodge if he intended staying in town for a while.

'It's still run by Roy Cole,' the pastor said. 'Roy's in his seventies but he's fit as a fiddle. It's quieter there than the Blue Star.'

Cole himself was serving behind the counter when Billy walked through the swing-doors. Four old-timers playing cards didn't even bother to look up as he passed. Maybe they were sleeping. Maybe it was the passage of time, or that the saloonkeeper's eyes weren't all that good; either way Cole didn't recognize the stranger, though Billy remembered him well enough.

'A room? Sure,' Cole said in reply to his enquiry. 'Will you be wanting to take a bath?'

'Yeah, right away if that's OK,' the gambler told him.

The old man nodded his head.

'I'll rustle up the maid,' he said. 'The water'll take half an hour or so.'

The doors swung open again and a small man came into the room. He was wearing shabby leather breeches and his check shirt was grimy. He stared in Billy's direction for a moment and the gambler wondered if they'd been acquainted in the past, but after a brief glance around the rest of the bar the man turned on his heels and went back out into the street.

Roy Cole insisted on showing his new guest up to his room.

'I like to keep on the move,' he told Billy between puffs as they reached the top of the stairs. 'That's your room over there, number five. Make yourself at home. The maid won't be long.'

Billy was stretched out on the bed when he heard a knock on the door. Surely the maid couldn't be as quick as that, or had he dozed off without knowing?

'Come on in,' he said. 'It ain't locked.'

The door opened to reveal a group of men standing in the corridor. They had all drawn their guns and were pointing them into the bedroom.

'That's the feller,' Billy heard one of them say. 'I'd recognize them fancy clothes anyplace.'

A tall, well-built man came into the room. He was wearing a tin star on his shirt.

'You're under arrest, mister,' he said.

Billy sat up on the bed and tried to sound more surprised than he felt.

'Under arrest?' he said. 'What for?'

'Horse-theft and murder,' the town marshal informed him. 'One wrong move and you're dead!'

EIGHT

Five men accompanied Billy Nash over to the jail-house: Nelmes the town marshal, and Wilbur Hawkins' quartet of hired gunfighters named Hixon, Walsh, Davidge and Lawthom. The carter who'd identified the gambler was allowed to slink away and celebrate his small reward in one of Cedar Hollow's saloons.

Although Clem Nelmes was the one wearing the badge it was Hixon, a lean, scarfaced man, who took control of proceedings once Lawthom had slammed the jailhouse door behind them.

'Tie him to the chair, Walsh,' he said. 'In case he tries to answer back.'

The form of questioning was a painful one. Hixon asked the questions while Davidge and Lawthom took turns to encourage their prisoner to answer by slapping him hard across the face

68

with the back of their hands. But try as they might, their combined effort failed to get Billy to change the main points of his story.

'I expected my brother Ty to be at the homestead,' the gambler explained over and over again. 'There was no sign of him or of anybody, so I spent the night by myself in the house and this morning I began walking to town. I'd got about halfway when I spotted the horse without a rider.'

'Why did you wheel away when you saw the wagon coming?' Hixon demanded.

'When I whistled the horse came to me,' Billy said. 'It didn't need much coaxing, like as if it knew it was lost. I was mighty glad to get on it; I was out on my feet. It was only when I saw the wagon that I realized I might be in trouble. I had no proof that I hadn't stolen the animal.'

'You still ain't got no proof,' Hixon reminded him. 'That horse belongs to a friend of ours called Potts. I'm gonna describe Potts to you to see if it jogs your memory.'

The description was accompanied by some more hard slaps that started blood flowing from the gambler's nostrils. Their violence only made him more determined.

'I don't know the feller,' he lied. 'I ain't never seen him.'

69

'Well, you better start praying that Potts does show up,' Hixon warned him. 'Otherwise you're gonna be swinging from a rope by this time tomorrow.'

When they'd finally had enough of listening to the same story, they untied his hands and threw him into one of the cells. He lay on the hard bunk for an hour or so, wondering how he was going to get out of this jam. When he opened them again he was aware of a man standing watching him through the cell bars. The man had filled out since he'd last seen him, and his face was puffy with drink but Billy recognized him nevertheless. It was his brother Ty.

The meeting with the lawyer Jeffrey Tomkinson was short and to the point. Wilbur Hawkins had worked out his strategy already. All that was needed was for Tomkinson to exchange his office shoes for a pair of riding boots for the next few days. It would do him good, though the lawyer's face was a picture when Hawkins gave him his orders.

'What, visit the homesteads?' he stammered. 'All of them?'

'That's right, all of them,' the banker repeated with a teasing grin. 'There are eleven of them altogether in the association, but you can forget Ty Nash's place; it's empty, and anyway he's on our side. If you get a move on you'll be finished in two or three days.'

When he'd briefed Tomkinson on the purpose of the visits to the homesteaders the banker went straight over to Miss Nellie's boarding-house where a buggy was already waiting as he'd ordered. He'd promised to take his fiancée out into the countryside for the afternoon and then back to his house for supper. It was a snap decision taken during their conversation at lunch; he wanted to prove to the girl that there were plenty of things to do in Cedar Hollow.

Mary Liddell looked radiant in a pink dress, with her golden hair tied in a light green bow. There was a bounce in her step as she approached the buggy.

'You make me feel like a young feller again, Miss Liddell,' Hawkins said with mock gallantry, then helped her up on to the seat.

'Dear, dear, Mr Hawkins,' she replied in kind. 'I always thought you *were* a young feller. Please don't disillusion me.'

After leaving town they followed a trail alongside the meandering river for a few miles before making for the hills.

'We need to gain some height,' the banker told his companion. 'So's I can show you just how lovely it is in these parts, and how fertile.'

Unfortunately, whenever they did reach a place of great beauty, Wilbur inevitably spoiled the magic of the moment by turning his thoughts to the economic and strategic value of the site.

'I look at this great land but I don't really see it as it is now,' he confided to the girl. 'I see it developing into towns and cities, with railroads and junctions, with huge cattle markets and thousands of head of cattle waiting to be carried in trucks rather than forced to tramp thousands of miles, dying and growing thin on the way so that by the end of the journey they're worth hardly anything at all.'

Mary Liddell said nothing, preferring to savour the wonder of the landscape. Hawkins took hold of her hand but his mood was by no means romantic.

'Cedar Hollow will have to face up to new challenges,' he declared. 'Otherwise the chance will be lost to make fortunes and wield influence.'

It was dark when the buggy drew up outside the imposing wooden house that the banker had built on the outskirts of town. The front door opened on cue and the maid came out to greet them. At the same moment the figure of a man detached itself from the shadows of the tall trees lining the boulevard.

'Mr Hawkins,' the man said in a slurred voice. 'Can I speak to you, please?'

The banker was embarrassed and annoyed by the intrusion. He turned at once to the girl and said, 'You go inside, my dear. I'll just see what he wants.'

His tone brooked no argument, and Mary allowed the maid to usher her through the door. Wilbur turned angrily on the intruder.

'What do you mean by coming to my house like this?' he demanded. 'Are you crazy?'

The man mumbled an apology, but he was too drunk to hold his peace.

'They've arrested my brother Billy, Mr Hawkins,' he said. 'They reckon he killed Potts. They're aiming to string him up.'

'Listen to me, Ty,' Hawkins said between clenched teeth. 'Anyone who kills one of my men gets strung up, d'you understand? Now, get out of my way or you'll wake up without a job tomorrow morning!'

NINE

At breakfast the next morning Wilbur Hawkins was still angry about Ty Nash's outburst the night before. Ty had better watch his step, he thought; Hixon and the others had a very low opinion of the so-called deputy marshal and it would only take a word from the banker for them to remove the drunk from the scene.

Marshal Nelmes had called at the house with a message for Hawkins while the banker had been driving his fiancée around the territory. Now, as he ate his bacon and eggs, Hawkins scribbled a note of reply which the maid could deliver at the jailhouse. He couldn't allow one of his hired guns simply to disappear without his retaliating. The message was short and unequivocal: *Hang him at noon.*

He arrived at the bank much later than usual.

His secretary Ann Forest was waiting outside his private office, looking unusually agitated.

'There've been several people trying to see you, Mr Hawkins,' she told him. 'None of them had appointments so I've arranged for them to come back later.' She glanced meaningfully at the office door. 'Pastor Jones was particularly obstinate,' she said apologetically. 'I had to let him into your office to wait for you.'

'That's OK, Miss Forest,' he assured her with a forced smile. 'It wouldn't be right to keep a man of the cloth waiting out in the street, would it? Thank you for dealing with the rest of them. I wonder why I'm so much in demand this morning?'

He was about to find out. Shad Jones' face was flushed.

'There's going to be a hanging in the square at noon,' the pastor burst out.

'Indeed?' the banker said innocently. 'Who's getting hanged?'

'Ty Nash's elder brother Billy,' Shad replied.

Wilbur walked over to his desk and took a fat cigar out of the box and lit it.

'What's this Billy Nash done?' he enquired.

'One of your men, Potts, has disappeared,' the pastor said. 'They're blaming it on Billy, but they haven't even given him a fair trial.'

'By *them*, I take it you mean Marshal Nelmes,' the banker suggested.

'They all took part in the arrest, Hixon and the rest of them,' Shad Jones said accusingly.

'But we do have a marshal in Cedar Hollow who decides what's lawful,' Hawkins persisted. 'Why don't you go and talk to him?'

'I did,' the pastor retorted. 'He said that if I wasn't happy I should go and see Tomkinson, but Tomkinson had already left town early this morning.'

Wilbur blew smoke at the ceiling. It was all working out quite nicely.

'Then that's that,' he remarked. 'I don't see how I can intervene. The marshal is one of your own folk, pastor, born and bred here in Cedar Hollow. I'm sure he's only doing what he thinks is best for the town.'

Shad Jones felt as if he'd run into a wall of resistance. Earlier he'd tried to get the lawman to admit that the planned execution was the banker's decision, but Nelmes had kept mum on the subject. He changed tack suddenly.

'Do you see much of Jay the timber-merchant nowadays, Wilbur?' he asked.

The banker raised his eyebrows. Had Jay been

opening his mouth about the ultimatum he'd given him?

'He was in here yesterday as it happens, Pastor,' he said. 'Any particular reason for you asking?'

'No, except that he was found dead in his bed this morning with both his wrists cut open,' Shad Jones replied. 'He'd killed himself.'

Wilbur found it difficult to look grief-stricken at the news. With Jay out of the way he'd have no problem foreclosing on the loan and taking possession of the timber-mill and the land it stood on.

'Well, that's a surprise to me,' he remarked. 'Why on earth should he kill himself?'

'According to his wife he came home agitated after his meeting with you,' the preacher said accusingly. 'He wasn't himself for the rest of the day.'

Hawkins sat down in the plush chair behind his desk. If Jay had left a suicide note Shad would have mentioned it by now.

'I had to put the facts to him, Pastor,' he said gravely. 'He was running his business into the ground. I told him to face up to reality, but I guess he found an easier way out.'

Shad Jones stood there in silence for a few

moments; his wife Emma would have known what to say to the banker, but the preacher felt much too depressed to get involved in an argument.

'Be that as it may,' he said at last, 'I take it that you're not going to help Billy Nash?'

Hawkins shuffled the papers in front of him.

'I can't, Pastor,' he lied. 'It's the law of the land and it's got to take its course.'

For the next few hours the banker worked undisturbed in his office. He was determined not to venture out on to the street until the hanging was over. If there was a storm brewing in Cedar Hollow over the affair, then Clem Nelmes could weather it; that's what the lawman was paid for.

But things did not work out as he'd planned. Just after midday his secretary Ann Forest burst into the room unceremoniously. Hawkins' first reaction was one of anger but when he saw that she'd been more or less propelled through the door by the gunslinger Hixon, he realized that something serious had happened.

'You've got to get over to the square,' Hixon informed him tersely. 'Everyone's going crazy. She's stopping us hanging Nash.'

The reference to *she* set an alarm bell off in the banker's brain. Without a word he snatched up his jacket and followed the gunslinger through the main room of the bank and out into the street. Here at the front of the building he could hear the commotion which had been inaudible from his office.

When they reached the crowded square Hixon used brute force to open a way for them through the onlookers. At the foot of the stairs leading up to the gallows' platform Hawkins raised his head and saw his fiancée Mary Liddell writhing, kicking and struggling in the embrace of town marshal Nelmes. Davidge, Lawthom and Walsh were on the platform too, guns drawn and warily eyeing the crowd in case someone else risked climbing up and trying to halt the execution. Of them all, Billy Nash seemed the least moved, but that was because his hands were tied securely behind his back and a noose was draped loosely around his neck.

Then the girl spotted the presence of Wilbur Hawkins at the foot of the steps and she gave up her unequal struggle against the burly lawman.

'Wilbur, Wilbur,' she gasped. 'Thank God you're here. They're going to hang him!'

The banker climbed the steps and laid his hand gingerly on her arm.

'Calm down, Mary,' he urged her. 'This is the way the law works out West. It's nothing to do with us.'

'But it is – it is!' she replied and he could see that she was wild-eyed with anger or fear. 'The man they're going to hang, he saved my life in Oakhill. Wire the marshal there and ask him. He'll tell you he's no murderer.'

Those among the crowd who remembered Billy Nash from the old days were stirred by the girl's words and began to express their approval of her actions. Billy Nash was from good Texan stock.

'Where the heck's Ty Nash?' one of them shouted. 'What kind of feller lets his own brother get strung up by a bunch of varmints like them?'

Even those who didn't know Billy Nash from Adam were now siding with the prisoner. Mary Liddell's courage had stirred them all up. As for Wilbur Hawkins, the banker hadn't got where he was by shirking decisions. He made a quick appraisal of the situation and accepted that to go ahead with the hanging would be a disaster. But there was a way to turn things to his advantage.

'In the light of what Miss Liddell tells us, Marshal Nelmes,' he proclaimed in a voice that carried across the square. 'I appeal for clemency for Mr Nash. Please do us all the favour of releasing him at once.'

His remark surprised the lawman so much that he slackened his hold on Mary Liddell. With feminine guile, the girl refrained from running over to where Billy Nash was standing. Instead, she made for Wilbur Hawkins and threw herself into his arms for protection. Meanwhile, a townsman had jumped up on to the platform and was cutting the cord binding the prisoner's wrists. The crowd were cheering loudly for Billy, Wilbur and Mary Liddell, and the gunslingers had sheathed their weapons.

The banker let his arm rest on his fiancée's shoulders as he surveyed the ecstatic throng of townsfolk. He allowed himself to savour this moment of popularity. He knew that it wasn't going to last.

TEN

Back in the banker's office, Mary Liddell trod carefully as she explained the motives for her unladylike behaviour in the square.

'During my journey in the stagecoach,' she said, 'I lodged overnight in a town called Oakhill. The hotel-owner asked me to sing a couple of songs, which I was happy to do. After the performance a ruffian attacked me for no reason except that he was drunk. He was a very violent man, Wilbur, and everybody was too afraid of him to come to my aid. I think he'd have done me serious harm if Mr Nash hadn't intervened. That's why I acted like I did just now. I'm sorry if I embarrassed you.'

The girl was shrewd enough to recognize another danger. If she praised Billy too much she risked making her fiancé suspicious and jealous.

'But it wasn't me who saved him back there,

Wilbur,' she added. 'If you hadn't shown up they'd have thrown me off the platform and gone ahead with the hanging. Now I can see how well respected you are in Cedar Hollow.'

Hawkins smiled modestly, but behind the affable façade he was doing some thinking of his own. This Billy Nash was quite unlike his brother Ty; he was fit and good-looking, and maybe he'd even been good enough to outgun Potts. That, together with the girl's obvious affection for him, made him an undesirable in town.

'Will you listen to me, Mary?' he asked her. 'You may not like what I'm going to say.'

She opened her blue eyes wide. Both she and Hawkins knew that neither of them was being completely sincere with the other, but it was a game that circumstances forced them to play.

'I'm listening, Wilbur,' she assured him.

'Potts, the man Nash is accused of killing, had friends in town. They are the fellers you tangled with just now. They're hard men, Mary, and they're not going to rest until they even the score with Billy Nash.'

'But they listened to you, Wilbur,' she pointed out with more than a hint of admiration in her voice. 'You could handle them.'

'I guess they did,' he admitted. 'But I'm not

going to be with them all the time. Sooner or later one of them is going to run into Billy Nash, and I cain't answer for the consequences.'

She fell silent, waiting for him to continue. She didn't mind what he came up with so long as Billy wasn't harmed.

'He'll have to leave town,' Hawkins said. 'It's the only way I can guarantee his safety.'

Her face broke into a smile of gratitude.

'You're right, Wilbur,' she told him. 'I'm sure he'll see sense. But please watch that no harm comes to him before he leaves.'

Out in the street she found a burly man in a clerical collar waiting for her.

'Excuse me, Miss Liddell,' he said. 'Could I have a word, please?'

They walked side by side the length of two blocks. Shad Jones was anxious to thank the girl for saving the life of his young friend Billy.

'I guess you performed a small miracle, Miss Liddell,' he commented. 'I went to see Wilbur Hawkins this morning to seek his help, and he showed no willingness to stop the hanging.'

The girl digested his words but said nothing. Wilbur was her fiancé, after all.

'Well, I just wanted to thank you, that's all,' the preacher went on. 'My family and the Nashes go back a long way; in fact, at one time I even thought that Billy's younger brother Ty might become my son-in-law, but that's not the way it worked out.' He pointed an arm towards the far end of the street. 'Do you see the church?' he said. 'Well, that's our house next to it. My wife Emma and my daughter Janie would be mighty pleased to make your acquaintance if you cared to call on us. If you ever need anything . . .'

She smiled at him; she was beginning to feel at home in Cedar Hollow.

'Thank you,' she said. 'I'll remember that.'

The banker's next meeting was not as congenial as the one he'd had with Mary Liddell. Ann Forest ushered Marshal Nelmes into his office, together with Hixon, the leader of the hired guns.

Clem Nelmes did all the talking for the first few minutes. He complained bitterly about Hawkins' volte-face over the proposed hanging of Billy Nash.

'You made me look real bad, Mr Hawkins,' he said, 'and foolish with it. I never wanted to hang Billy in the first place, but it was your decision so I went along with it. Then you changed your mind because of that . . .'

His voice trailed off as he saw the warning glint

in the banker's eye. But even if the lawman didn't dare say so, everyone knew that it was the girl's intervention that had caused all the trouble. Even folk who could barely remember Billy Nash had been moved by Mary Liddell's courage and determination. Her action had made a laughing stock of the men who'd been doing their duty on the scaffold that morning.

Wilbur Hawkins turned to Hixon. He could detect an unspoken contempt in the gunslinger's gaze, and he didn't like it.

'Well, spit it out, Hixon,' he snapped. 'Are you agreeing with Nelmes here?'

Hixon merely shrugged his shoulders. The girl was a complication, but there was always a remedy for complications. He and the other hired guns would continue to do their job regardless of the difficulties. If the girl insisted on getting in the way, then she was the one who'd suffer.

'It was my mistake,' the banker admitted unexpectedly. 'I didn't realize how high feelings were running over the hanging. I've got plans for this town and for you boys as well, and I don't want them ruined by a stupid mistake.'

Hixon spoke for the first time.

'If Potts is dead,' he said coldly, 'somebody oughta pay for it.'

'That's a big *if*, Hixon,' Hawkins remarked. 'But let it serve as a lesson. Potts always was a loose cannon, going off by himself and looking for trouble. From now on you've got to keep the gang together, keep them under control.'

He turned to the lawman.

'I want you to see to it that Billy Nash leaves town at once,' he said. 'And warn him not to come back. You'd better take Ty with you.'

'Ty?'

'That's right. If the townsfolk see Billy being escorted out of Cedar Hollow by Hixon's men, they'll suspect the worst. If they see his brother tagging along everything will be OK.'

Billy Nash was standing at the counter of the Mexican Trail saloon when the marshal caught up with him.

'You're leaving town, Billy,' the lawman announced. 'We've got a horse saddled up outside. You'll get your gunbelt back when you're clear of town. It's for your own good.'

The handful of customers watched while Nelmes waited for Billy to go up to his room and collect his few belongings. Billy raised no objections; he'd had one lucky escape already and he didn't want to push his luck any further. Before he followed the marshal out of the saloon, the gambler asked saloonkeeper Roy Cole how much he owed him for the bath.

'Nothing,' the old-timer replied. 'I can remember your pa coming to Cedar Hollow when he was a young man. *Hasta luego*, and good luck.'

Ty Nash was waiting outside with the horses. He looked bleary-eyed with drink and he didn't say a word when his brother appeared with the town marshal. The three men rode in silence for almost an hour in the warm afternoon sunshine before Clem Nelmes drew rein.

'This is where you get down, Billy,' he said. 'Cedar Hollow don't provide horses for killers. I'll drop your gunbelt when we've put a couple of hundred yards between us.'

Billy dismounted with a sinking feeling in his stomach. He wasn't concerned for himself; he'd been in worse predicaments before. What hurt was his brother's apparent indifference to him, like as if they were total strangers.

'Is that it, Ty?' he asked suddenly. 'Don't you have anything to say to me?'

Clem Nelmes ignored the remark and wheeled his horse away. Ty hesitated for a moment, then dismounted awkwardly and walked over towards where his elder brother was standing.

'Since you're asking, Billy,' he said in a voice

throbbing with anger, 'I guess I do have a few things to say to you. For a start, you're a lousy sonofabitch for not coming home and helping out after Ma, Pa and James died; and you're a sonofabitch for what you've done since you are back. You're a no-good horse-thief, Billy, and I was stupid enough to go out on a limb and speak up for you to Mr Hawkins the banker. I owe Hawkins everything and I couldn't blame him if he took it all away from me like he threatened to if I didn't shut my goddam fool mouth. And now good old Billy Nash is getting away scot free for everything he's done, yet folk are still going to blame me for not trying to save that useless neck of yours.'

Billy listened to his brother's words with a growing sense of sadness; sadness for his own failings which Ty had rightly pointed out, but sadness also for Ty, who was a shadow of the youngster he'd grown up with. The Nashes had always been a proud, independent family, but Ty had sold out to a man like Wilbur Hawkins who owned people like ranchers owned cattle.

'That's OK then, Ty,' he commented softly. 'Maybe you'll feel better now that you've got it off your chest. Maybe you'll stop feeling sorry for yourself. That would be a start, I reckon.'

Drunk as he was, Ty took a moment or two to

get his brother's meaning. When he did, his cheeks burned red.

'Don't you go telling me how to live my life, Billy,' he said. 'The days are long gone when I went to you for advice.'

Clem Nelmes could feel the tension in the air and his hand dropped on to the handle of his .45. He couldn't let Ty gun down his unarmed brother. How would he explain that to Wilbur Hawkins and, more importantly, all Billy's new-found supporters in Cedar Hollow?

But Ty had no intention of drawing his gun. Instead, he unbuckled his belt and let it drop to the ground.

'So here we are, Billy,' he said, 'just like the good old days; ready to use our fists to settle our differences.'

Clem Nelmes shook his head in disbelief. Ty clearly didn't realize how far he'd let himself go in the intervening years. Judging by the contrasting condition of the two brothers, the lawman wouldn't have bet a cent against a hundred dollars on Ty beating Billy in a fistfight.

However, Ty was too worked up to calculate the odds. He lumbered forward stiffly and swung a haymaker right at his elder brother's head. Billy saw it coming a mile off, yet he took no evasive action. When the punch landed it shook him to the core but he didn't even try to raise his hands.

Ty swung again, with the left this time. It was less cumbersome than the previous effort and it crashed against Billy's unprotected cheekbone. This time he stumbled and Ty closed in and jabbed him solidly in the midriff. Billy coughed and sank to the ground. Nelmes was expecting Ty to back off at this point but the younger brother's temper was inflamed. As Billy rolled himself into a ball on the ground Ty kept kicking him in the ribs and on the thighs.

Nelmes had seen enough; when his shouts went unheeded he drew his Colt and fired once into the air.

'Goddam you, Ty,' he yelled. 'I promised Wilbur I'd see Billy safely out of the territory. Do I have to kill you to keep my word?'

Blood was trickling out of the cuts and abrasions on Billy Nash's face and body. Ty turned away suddenly and made for his horse. When he'd mounted up he fixed his stricken brother with a look that bore no pity or regret.

'Next time, Billy,' he said coldly. 'Next time . . .'

The gambler felt his head being raised from the ground and tepid water lapping on to his lips and chin. He opened his mouth and drank greedily.

'Steady on, young feller,' a voice cautioned him. 'If you ain't careful you're gonna bring it all up again.'

He opened his eyes and saw a ginger-haired man kneeling by his side. The sun was quite low in the sky; he must have been lying there for a few hours.

'Say, if my eyes ain't playing games with me, ain't you one of them Nashes who used to farm in these parts? I reckon I can recall you when you was a young lad.'

Through swollen lips Billy confirmed his identity to the Samaritan.

'That's right – Billy Nash,' the ginger man said happily. 'Why our farms are only five miles or so apart, though yours is in a pretty bad way nowadays. A little like you, I guess.'

Billy managed to hoist himself into a sitting position, though every movement was painful to him.

'You'd better come on back to my place,' the man said. 'D'you remember me now? I'm Doug Paine and I got one son left on the farm, Horace. He's younger than you; he was just a kid when you marched off to the war.'

Even in his present weakened condition Billy

didn't want his bad luck to spread to the Paine homestead like a contagion. Nelmes and his cronies wouldn't look kindly on anyone who offered him help.

'I want to go back to my folks' place,' he told Paine. 'I gotta rest up a while.'

'You sure do need to,' Paine remarked. 'D'you want to tell me what happened?'

His question was met by silence. He decided not to press the point.

'OK, son,' he said. 'But first you'll have to come back with me 'cos you ain't in no condition to walk to your place from here. I've got a spare horse at the moment, 'cos Horace has gone and broke a bone in his leg. You can borrow it for a while. Us homesteaders still stick together, Billy, just like they did when your ma and pa were still alive.'

ELEVEN

Although he was intent on finding and gunning down Billy Nash to avenge the death of his cousin Cab, Josh Barlow was also eager to make easy money whenever the opportunity presented itself. The township of Mackay, a few miles inside the Texas border, seemed to offer just the sort of opportunity the outlaw was looking for.

Mackay was a stagnant little settlement that had failed to develop beyond a double-row of wooden dwellings set on the fertile plain of east Texas. It boasted one ramshackle saloon and a single general-purpose store. The Barlow brothers chose the former as the starting point of their visit. It was just after midday that they tethered their horses to the rail and went inside to slake their thirst.

The place was dark, drab and dingy and there

was as much dust on the furniture as in the street outside. The bartender was bald and plump, with a red complexion and a chest that wheezed like a punctured accordion. They'd hardly had time to order a couple of beers when he began explaining to them that he hadn't been in good health since he'd caught pneumonia at the siege of Yorktown in '62.

'I was good as dead already when them Yankees over-ran the place,' he said. 'I just don't know how I survived the rest of the war in their prison camps 'fore I was set free and told to find my own way home.'

Apart from his chestiness he seemed in fine fettle despite his past ordeals. The saloon was empty and he was obviously glad to have someone to talk to. Josh Barlow decided to take advantage of the circumstances and get straight to the point.

' 'Tain't much of a town you got here, mister,' he commented bluntly. 'You ain't even got a bank.'

The bartender shook his head sadly.

'Time's kinda passed Mackay by,' he replied philosophically. 'Of course, the war didn't help none; just when it seemed like the place might take off and become prosperous all the young men had to leave for the army, and lots of them never made it back again. They even took me and I wasn't young by no means.'

'You always empty like this?' Dill Barlow enquired suddenly.

'Nope, not always,' the bartender informed him. 'We get farmers and cowhands in on Saturday nights and maybe on Sunday afternoons the menfolk come in after the church service. Then there's market day once a month and—'

'How do folk borrow money in these parts?' Josh Barlow broke in. 'It ain't no wonder you got no businesses here.'

'Jack Law's the nearest thing you'll find to a banker,' the red-faced man replied. 'He organizes a small farming cooperative from his store along the street. You cain't miss it; it's the only store in town. If Jack Law ain't got what you want, you got a forty-mile journey ahead of you at least, whatever direction you head off in.'

Josh swallowed the remainder of his beer and signalled to his younger brother to do likewise. Taking their leave of the bartender they walked out into the street. Josh turned to Dill and said tersely: 'I'm gonna pay Jack Law a visit. It wasn't worth holding up that saloonkeeper. I guess he ain't got two cents to rub together.'

Dill nodded his head. He only disagreed with Josh when the latter was in a reckless mood, but judging by the emptiness of the street the general store was going to be a pushover.

They walked the horses casually through the tiny settlement until they reached Jack Law's general store. Both outlaws kept their eyes peeled but nobody even came to a window to watch them go by.

'Am I going in with you, Josh?' the younger Barlow enquired.

'Nope, I can handle this on my own,' Josh assured him. 'You stay outside with the horses, and whistle if there's any problem.'

The hinge of the door creaked as the outlaw went inside. A middle-aged, well-dressed lady was standing near the window, examining some curtain material in the sunlight. She gave the newcomer a cursory glance, then turned her attention back to the cloth in her hand.

A thin, round-shouldered man was standing behind the counter holding a large box that probably contained samples he was about to show the lady customer. As he manoeuvred the box on to an empty stretch of counter top, Josh Barlow strode purposefully up to him, drawing his Colt as he walked. He raised the gun and levelled it at the shopkeeper's head.

'Get over to the till and empty the money into a bag for me, mister,' he ordered. 'Do like I say and neither you nor the lady is gonna get hurt.'

Without saying a word Jack Law moved smoothly over to the till. The woman had frozen at the outlaw's words; her hands were shaking so much that the material she'd been holding fell to the floor with a sound like a sigh.

Outside in the street the front door of a house opened and a small man in his early forties emerged. His eyes locked on Dill Barlow for a moment as if he was trying to work out whether he knew him or not. Deciding that he didn't, the townsman nodded and Dill returned the compliment rather nervously. The man carried on walking in the direction of a corral at the end of the row of buildings.

Inside the store Jack Law was opening the drawer of the till. It was pretty full of coins and dollar bills but the shopkeeper ignored them and reached for the small revolver he also kept there. From where he was standing Josh Barlow couldn't see the inside of the till, but from her angled vantage point at the window the lady customer saw everything that was happening and she let out an involuntary, stifled scream.

In the silence of the sleepy township the shot rang out like a peal of thunder. The man who was on his way to the corral spun around, with a look of astonishment on his face. Then he began to run back towards the store. Dill Barlow had no choice in the matter; he drew his gun and pumped two slugs into the man's stomach from ten yards' range. The man fell forward on to his face and lay there quite still.

Inside the store, the woman was still screaming despite Josh Barlow's threats to kill her if she didn't shut up. Silently, Dill urged his brother to get on with it and come out of the store. In the meantime, he'd mounted up, in case it was the shopkeeper who'd triumphed, not Josh. But finally Josh did emerge, clutching a cloth bag that was stuffed with money.

'Get up, for God's sake,' Dill said. 'Our luck cain't hold for ever!'

Josh didn't need any coaxing. He leapt into the saddle and spurred his horse viciously. Dill felt a sense of relief as they sped past the corral, then he heard a shot somewhere behind them, and his brother gasped with pain.

'Where've they got you, Josh?' he enquired anxiously.

'In the thigh,' Josh replied through clenched teeth. 'I'll be OK.'

They rode hard for miles until they were confident that there was no immediate danger of pursuit. It would take a small place like Mackay some time to round up enough men to form a posse. Dill bound up the wound as well as he could with a strip of cloth torn from his own spare shirt. The bullet didn't need to be cut out; it had gone straight through the flesh, leaving two painful holes in its wake.

'I reckon we should head south for Mexico, Josh,' Dill said cautiously. 'This is bound to slow you up for a while. Why don't we just forget that feller who killed Cab?'

His elder brother gritted his teeth against the pain.

'We'll keep following the route the stage took,' he replied stubbornly. 'Nash has to get off sooner or later.'

TWELVE

Despite what he'd said she knew that he'd come now that her husband was making a tour of the homesteads. It was dusk when her black maid, Mona, came into the parlour and announced that Wilbur Hawkins was in the hallway, asking to see her.

'Show him in, Mona,' Kathryn Tomkinson said. 'Oh, by the way, Mrs Booth should have finished that crochet-work for me by now. Take ten dollars from my purse and call over to see her, will you? There's no reason for you to hurry back.'

The maid nodded, her expression inscrutable. It was owing to Mona's loyalty and discretion that her mistress's affair with the banker had remained a secret.

It felt so good to feel her lover's body pressing against hers in the spacious bed that she was forced to share with her husband each night. The lawyer worshipped her but he was no man. Wilbur, on the other hand, was confident, dynamic, ruthless; the kind of man I should have married, she thought ruefully.

This evening Wilbur was less talkative than usual but no less efficient. Kathryn was sure that he must be tiring already of that empty-headed young slut who'd humiliated him publicly by defending that common criminal, Billy Nash.

'Take your time, Wilbur; take your time,' she chided him good-humouredly. 'I've told you Jeffrey isn't coming back tonight. He's staying at the Sheppards' ranch; he says it will save him time in the long run. He doesn't much like this latest work you've given him, but I think it's a wonderful idea. For once you can stay overnight, so long as you leave before daybreak.'

He relaxed his efforts for a moment.

'I can't stay,' he told her. 'I have to be back before supper. I have an engagement.'

He averted his eyes as he spoke and she felt a cold fury overwhelm her.

'It's her, isn't it?' she said accusingly. 'You're going back to *her*!'

He tried to hold her, but she pulled away from him and swung her feet onto the floor.

'After all she's done to you, you're still going through with the marriage?' she asked, wrapping her silk dressing-gown around her naked body. 'If you're so worried that she'll find out about us, why don't you question her about that killer whose life she saved? Don't you realize you're the laughing-stock of Cedar Hollow?'

He lay there, waiting for her to simmer down and get back into bed. When she didn't, he sighed and reached for his clothes.

'You're making things very difficult, dear,' he told her. 'I've already explained that we need to be careful. It's got nothing to do with Mary Liddell.'

She was still sitting silently on the bed when he left a few minutes later, her face set hard, but with a trace of moisture on her eyelashes.

The interior of the cabin was cool and a welcome relief from the heat of the afternoon. Doug Paine drew a wooden chair from under the gnarled table and bade the lawyer sit down and make himself comfortable. Jeffrey Tomkinson obliged, placing his leather briefcase within easy reach of his hand. He glanced at the bed in the corner of the room. A boy aged about fifteen was propped up on a pile of pillows. The odour pervading the room indicated that the boy's clothing or the bedclothes, or both, were long overdue for a wash. The boy glanced at the visitor then turned his attention back to the carbine he was in the process of oiling and cleaning.

'That's my son Horace,' the homesteader informed the lawyer proudly. 'All he can do is clean the guns so long as his leg is busted.'

'Has he seen the doc?' Tomkinson enquired.

'Nope,' Doug Paine replied. 'Folks like us cain't afford no doc. But I learned to set bones from my pa. Pa was a great healer and I inherited some of it. I'll have my boy walking again in a couple of weeks.'

The lawyer reached for the leather case and opened it. He produced a slim document and laid it on the table.

'That's what I've come to see you about, Mr Paine,' he said smoothly. 'Money.'

The homesteader gave an ironic little laugh.

'Money,' he chortled. 'I hope you ain't wasted your time coming looking for money on my place!'

Tomkinson assumed a serious, businesslike expression.

'Not to look for money here, Mr Paine,' he corrected the homesteader. 'I'm here to bring you money.'

Doug Paine stopped laughing; he was wary

now. He wasn't an educated person, but neither did he lack intelligence. Long, hard years of contact with the soil had endowed him with plenty of common sense and caution. He didn't trust townsfolk much, and especially not lawyers or the like.

'You belong to an association of homesteaders formed by Mr Wilbur Hawkins shortly after he opened his bank,' Tomkinson said.

'Sure, I remember that,' Paine agreed. 'Only it ain't ever brought me a cent.'

'That's because you're too proud a man to ask for help,' the lawyer pointed out. 'Other homesteaders have enjoyed substantial loans at extremely low rates of interest.'

'I don't want no loans,' Paine commented, spitting into the empty grate as he spoke. 'That's another thing my pa taught me.'

Tomkinson managed to smile thinly, but not without an effort. He'd had a hard few days travelling around persuading the other homesteaders to accept Hawkins' new deal.

'We're not talking loans, Doug,' he said coaxingly. 'We're talking of a new set-up where you'll get payments as a right, not loans.'

'Listen to what he has to say, Pa,' the boy said suddenly from the corner of the room. 'You always tell me there ain't no harm in listening.'

'Mr Hawkins intends to set up a company of homesteaders working in cooperation with the bank at Cedar Hollow,' the lawyer explained. 'There are eleven homesteads concerned, including yours if you wish to join, and each will have a share in the total profits.'

'What about Hawkins?' Paine asked suspiciously. 'Will he have a share?'

The lawyer beamed at him; this was the kind of interest he'd hoped Doug Paine would show.

'The bank will own ten shares in the company,' he explained. 'And each homestead will have one share, making eleven in all to cast against the bank if there's any disagreement. That way the united votes of the homesteaders will always overrule the bank, despite the fact that it's the bank that's prepared to finance the venture from the start.'

'Sounds fair, Pa,' Horace Paine chirped up from his corner. 'What about the money you promised us, mister?'

'Mr Hawkins will make an initial investment of one hundred dollars in each smallholding,' the lawyer promised. 'That can pay for tools, seeds, or even doctor's fees.'

'Pa . . .'

'Shut up, son, and let me think,' his father said sharply, and the boy fell silent.

Doug Paine took his time, and Tomkinson waited with growing impatience. The homesteader could foresee the ease with which Wilbur Hawkins would cast his block vote and the difficulty which the other members might have in reaching a common agreement, especially if the banker and his crony Tomkinson resorted to bribery to divide them.

'What happens if I don't join, Mr Tomkinson?' he asked at length.

The lawyer tapped the document spread out before him.

'This has been drawn up on the basis of a twenty-one share company, Doug,' he replied. 'Everyone else has agreed to the deal, but if you pull out the document may as well be torn up. Of course, nobody will get the hundred-dollar handout, and you aren't going to be very popular in these parts.'

The homesteader shrugged his shoulders philosophically.

'Well, I ain't signing,' he said flatly. 'So you'd better start tearing.'

THIRTEEN

Billy Nash had every reason to be grateful to Doug Paine, who had not only lent him a horse but had also given him two sacks of vegetables, some salted beef and a rifle to hunt game. Despite his injuries and despite his memories Billy was not unhappy to be back on his parents' land; he needed to rest up for a few days and then decide what to do next.

A couple of days later he received some welcome, if unexpected, visitors. Janie Jones, the preacher's daughter, turned up at the farm together with Mary Liddell. The girls were equally surprised to see him.

'Wilbur bought me a horse so that I could go riding with Janie,' Mary explained to him. 'Janie's parents have been really good to me since you left town. I asked if we could ride out and see the place where you were brought up, Billy. I didn't expect to find you here; Wilbur told me that the marshal and your brother Ty had escorted you safely out of the territory for your own good.'

Billy hoped that she wouldn't draw attention to the cuts and bruises on his face and he was glad when neither girl mentioned the matter.

'I guess I'm far enough from town not to bother anybody,' Billy replied. 'Though I'd be grateful if you'd both forget that you've seen me.'

'But I'll have to tell Ma and Pa,' Janie protested. 'They've been worried sick about you. They thought that maybe Nelmes had—'

'Your ma and pa are just fine, Janie,' Billy said. 'I wish I could say the same about everyone in Cedar Hollow.'

The visit was a short one since the girls had to get back to town, but Janie Jones was intrigued by the close understanding which Billy and Mary Liddell seemed to have. On their way back to Cedar Hollow she commented: 'Maybe I'm talking out of turn, Mary, but I think Billy Nash likes you a lot.'

The young singer blushed; it made her feel guilty to think that it was a present from her fiancé that had made the meeting possible.

'We do get on well together,' she conceded

cagily. 'That's why I'm so grateful to Wilbur for saving Billy's life.'

Janie Jones was harbouring thoughts of her own. Seeing Billy again had reminded her of happier days when she and Ty Nash had also had an understanding; but that was long ago, before Ty had fallen in with men like Wilbur Hawkins and his hired guns.

Lawyer Jeffrey Tomkinson looked weary and downcast when Ann Forest showed him into the office at the rear of the bank. Tomkinson had been home, bathed and changed from his riding clothes; but though he was relieved to be back among civilized folk after days on the range he still couldn't disguise his disappointment that his mission had proved a failure.

Wilbur Hawkins waited patiently until the lawyer had finished recounting his experiences before making a comment of his own.

'So, everybody signed except Doug Paine,' he said.

'And Ty Nash,' Tomkinson replied. 'I didn't even call at his place; it's been empty for years.'

'The marshal got Nash to sign last night in the saloon,' Hawkins informed him. 'So it's all tied up nicely.'

The lawyer stared at him. Wilbur didn't seem to understand. Hadn't he explained himself clearly?

'Doug Paine didn't sign; he refused,' he said again. 'That invalidates all the contracts.'

The banker pointed to the leather case Tomkinson had brought with him.

'Open it up, Jeffrey,' he said. 'Let's see the signatures.'

His visitor did as he was told and pulled out a sheaf of documents.

'This is Paine's,' he explained, 'the unsigned one. The next one is . . .'

Hawkins pushed the first contract to one side, then began opening the others. He stopped at the third or fourth.

'What's this?' he asked, pointing to the letter *X* that had been scribbled on the last line.

The lawyer studied the document for a moment.

'That's Wheelan's signature,' he said. 'He can't write. There are a few more like that; they're perfectly legal.'

He glanced at the banker. Wilbur Hawkins was grinning like a wolf.

'That's all we need on Doug Paine's contract,' Hawkins pointed out. 'Just an *X*. D'you get my drift, Jeffrey?'

The lawyer was tired after his long trip; but not too tired to spot the flaw in the banker's reasoning.

'If you do that, Paine will kick up a stink,' he said. 'He won't take it lying down. He's a cussed old varmint.'

Hawkins replaced the contracts in the leather case, but left the unsigned one on the table. When he handed the case to his visitor he was still smiling.

'I'll send the boys round to see him,' he said. 'Maybe they'll be able to change his mind.'

Davidge, Lawthom and Walsh waited impatiently for Hixon to get back from his meeting with Wilbur Hawkins over at the bank. They were seated around a table in the Blue Star saloon, and Hixon's poker hand still lay face-down where he'd thrown it when he'd heard that the banker needed to talk to him pronto.

Life in Cedar Hollow was monotonous for the four gunslingers since Marshal Clem Nelmes, whom they were supposed to back up in the event of trouble, kept things pretty much under control in the township. Now, however, they could sense that there was something in the air, that they were at last going to be called upon to put their skills to use.

The main door of the saloon swung open and Lawthom's head shot round expectantly. But it wasn't Hixon, only Ty Nash. Ty's shirt was half out of his breeches and his gait was unsteady. Lawthom noticed that the drunk had forgotten to pin on the tin star he normally wore, and he pointed the fact out to his two companions, just to relieve the boredom.

'It don't make no difference,' Davidge commented sarcastically. 'Ty won't make a lawman as long as he's got a hole in his ass!'

The remark tickled Walsh and he laughed out loud. Ty Nash turned and stared at him, unaware that the laughter was directed at him. Walsh reached into his breast-pocket for a coin; he threw it straight at the deputy marshal, but so low that Ty was bound to fumble it.

'Get yourself a drink, Marshal,' Walsh said mockingly. 'Sorry my aim's so poor.'

The coin had rolled under a nearby table. For a moment it looked as if the drunk was going to stand on his dignity, but the offer was too good to pass up, so Ty went down on his hands and knees to retrieve the money. As he was getting up again, clutching the coin in his hand, Lawthom pretended to help him but actually leaned heavily on his shoulder so that Ty crashed down again on to the floor.

'For Chrissake steady yourself, Ty,' he jeered. 'I ain't never seen you this drunk before.'

The deputy marshal hauled himself upright and fixed Lawthom with a baleful stare. He was more or less certain that the gang were baiting him, but he was less certain as to what he should do about it.

Then Hixon strode in through the swing-doors. Ignoring Ty completely, he addressed his three partners.

'Get saddled up,' he told them. 'We're going for a ride.'

The gunslingers rose to their feet. Ty placed a hand on the nearest table to steady himself.

'D'you want me to ride along with you, Hixon?' he enquired hopefully.

Hixon didn't even glance in his direction.

'The day I need you, Nash,' he said coldly. 'I'll be in deep trouble.'

Doug Paine was pouring water from a wooden pail into a long trough as a half-dozen squealing piglets pressed against his legs in their eagerness to slake their thirst.

'Steady on now,' he chided them. 'There's enough for everyone. When did you ever see the well run dry? I never did, and I been here nigh on forty years.'

The horsemen were almost upon him before he heard them. They were strangers, but he recognized at once the kind of men they were. He'd left his gun inside the house and he felt suddenly naked without it. Not that he'd be wise to use it against odds like these, but it would be a comfort to feel it at his hip anyways.

Hixon was the first to speak.

'You got any objection to us watering our horses?' he asked the homesteader.

'None at all,' Paine assured him. 'There's plenty where that came from.'

The four riders dismounted and allowed the horses to make their own way to the trough. According to the unwritten law of hospitality Doug Paine knew he ought to ask them into the house, but somehow he didn't think this was a social visit.

Hixon slapped the dust from his breeches with his Stetson.

'I hear Tomkinson the lawyer came to see you the other day,' he said.

'That's right,' the homesteader agreed. 'Tomkinson was here.'

'That's why we've come,' Hixon explained. 'Mr Hawkins don't think that the lawyer explained things properly to you. I've got a contract in my saddle-bag for you to sign and a hundred dollars to make it worth your while.'

Doug Paine didn't believe in beating about the bush, whomever he was talking to.

'You're wasting your time, mister,' he said bluntly. 'I already told Tomkinson I ain't signing.'

He was thinking quickly as he spoke; if he could make it back to the house he'd be much less vulnerable. He decided on a gamble; he turned his back on the gunslingers and began to walk casually towards the safety of the door.

'Look at me when I'm talking to you,' Hixon said sharply, but Doug Paine just kept on walking.

Walsh had already drawn his .45. He exchanged glances with Hixon, who nodded his head almost imperceptibly. The sound of the shot sent the piglets scattering in all directions. The homesteader's body tensed for a second and then his legs crumpled under him. He twitched once or twice as he lay on the ground, then all movement ceased.

Walsh re-sheathed his Colt. It had been so easy to earn his share of the hundred dollars. Davidge went over to his horse and began to check the

116

girth as if nothing had happened. Meanwhile, Lawthom had decided to take a look inside the house. Hixon thought nothing of it until a second explosion seemed to shake the walls of the building.

'Jeez, what's that?' Davidge called out as his horse reared in fright.

Hixon didn't bother to answer. Avoiding the doorway, he ran around the side of the house until he came to an open window. He risked a peek inside and saw a young lad propped up on the bed, holding a shotgun in his hands. If Lawthom was still alive he was keeping pretty quiet about it.

Hixon didn't fancy getting his head blown off so he pressed his back against the solid wall of the building and waited. Walsh was calling his name but he didn't answer. It was up to the others to make their move.

An age seemed to go by before anything happened, then he heard shots round at the front of the house and the shotgun exploded again. This time Hixon accepted the risk; he moved back to the window and saw that the boy was pointing the shotgun at the open doorway. He fired once, twice, and the boy screamed with pain. Hixon didn't stop firing until the hammer clicked on an empty chamber.

When Walsh and Davidge ventured inside, they found Lawthom dead with a gaping hole in his chest. Young Horace Paine was a raw, bleeding corpse tangled up with the filthy bed-linen.

'The sonofabitch,' Walsh said savagely. 'The goddam stupid sonofabitch!'

Hixon wasn't sure if the gunslinger was referring to Lawthom or the boy. It made no difference; with Lawthom dead there was no way they could deny their involvement in these latest killings.

FOURTEEN

Billy Nash let the logs he was carrying fall to the
ground when he saw pastor Shad Jones ride past
the corral and dismount by the side of the barn.
There was no mistaking the preacher, even from a
distance; he wore a distinctive grey jacket and
white shirt in all weathers and he rode erect as if
he was standing in the pulpit of his church.

Leaving his horse in the shade of the barn Shad
walked over to where Billy was working.

'Have you heard about your neighbour Doug
Paine?' he asked.

'Doug?' Billy wiped the sweat from his forehead. 'Nope. What's he been up to?'

The preacher's face was sombre as he replied,
'He got himself killed a few days ago. We're not
really sure when. It was only by chance that some
friends of his called over to see how the boy was.

119

They found them both dead – gunned down.'

Billy felt a lump in his throat. Doug Paine had been good to him, had staked him out. He thought about the boy, Horace, who'd been too ill to leave his bed and the anger welled up inside him.

'Did they get a chance to fight back?' he inquired.

'The shotgun had been fired,' Shad replied. 'There were pellets and blood everywhere. In the meantime, one of Hixon's men has gone missing, so folk are beginning to put two and two together.'

The two men walked over to the house and went inside.

'Why should Hixon's gang do a thing like that?' Billy asked. 'I thought they hung out in town doing Wilbur Hawkins' dirty work.'

The preacher accepted the mug of water Billy handed him. It tasted sweet after the ride. When he'd washed down the dust he explained about the contracts the homesteaders had signed.

'As soon as the news about the Paines broke, some of the homesteaders came to see me to ask for advice,' he said. 'They're pretty worried about the future of their properties. I've seen Hawkins and Tomkinson and they've agreed to hold a meeting of shareholders in the church hall tomorrow afternoon at two.'

120

Billy looked at him quizzically. The preacher had ridden a long way to keep him informed.

'Where do I fit in?' he asked. 'I ain't signed no contract.'

'Everyone I talk to mentions your name, Billy,' Shad Jones replied. 'They think you'd be a good man to have on their side. I told them that you probably wouldn't want to get involved, but they wanted me to ask you all the same.'

Billy sat there in silence for a few moments.

'It's a hard one, Pastor,' he said. 'I'll need to sleep on it.'

The church hall was filled not only with home-steaders and their families but also with their friends among the townsfolk. Word had spread quickly that Hawkins and Tomkinson were up to some skulduggery and feelings were already running high.

Hawkins had told Hixon and the other gunslingers to be close at hand but out of sight in case the situation turned ugly. However, he was confident that Tomkinson's legal expertise and his own smooth cunning would keep things under control.

Pastor Shad Jones went into the hall a few minutes before the meeting was due to commence. He'd been waiting outside in the vain hope that Billy Nash would show up. One of the Nashes was there – Ty – seated at the main table with Marshal Clem Nelmes, Wilbur Hawkins and Tomkinson the lawyer.

As soon as the banker asked for comments to open the discussion there was a hubbub of noise as the homesteaders competed to make themselves heard. Hawkins and Tomkinson were being accused of every crime from theft to murder. Shad Jones could see that this was getting them nowhere, so he called for silence and then proceeded to air their grievances in measured tones.

'These people here are worried that their lands may be sold if you or anyone else gains a majority holding in the company, Mr Hawkins,' he explained.

The banker reached for a copy of the contract and held it aloft.

'There are no plans to sell any land,' he replied. 'But even if land was sold everybody would get a fair share of the proceeds. That's written into the contract.'

The homesteaders stifled their protests. All eyes were turned on the preacher, including Hawkins', which were filled with venom. One day he'd make Jones regret siding with this rabble.

'But let's imagine that this present company was taken over by another for let's say a hundred dollars or so a share,' Jones continued slowly so that everyone could follow his logic. 'The second company could make a huge profit at a later date by selling out to a cattle baron or even a railroad outfit.'

The banker almost choked on his cigar. Shad had hit the nail on the head at his first attempt. Then a door opened at the back of the hall and Billy Nash slipped in almost unnoticed. Ty saw him, though, and the younger brother's eyes narrowed into slits.

Realizing that Wilbur Hawkins was momentarily at a loss for words, Tomkinson the lawyer decided to intervene.

'That's all empty conjecture, Pastor,' he said, 'and quite irrelevant to this discussion. The company we've formed is perfectly legal as it stands; so nothing can be changed by talking, it's all down in black and white.'

'What about Doug Paine?' a voice shouted from the middle of the hall. 'Doug's dead, so that means that the company's dead too.'

The lawyer shook his head emphatically.

'Doug signed the contract in my presence days

before he died,' he said without blinking an eyelid. 'His signature is here for anyone to see. Each and every one of the contracts is properly drawn up and signed. If you can prove otherwise, I'll accept that they're all worthless and that the company no longer exists.'

He sat back in his chair with a self-satisfied smile on his face. The room fell silent and even Shad Jones felt that they were beaten. Billy Nash chose that very moment to speak out.

'Well, at least one of the contracts is worthless,' he said in a loud voice. 'I mean the one relating to my property.'

His brother Ty rose from his seat, his face flushed with anger. Clem Nelmes pulled him forcibly down again, but still Ty managed to blurt out a few words.

'Your property,' he growled. '*Your* property!'

'That's right, Ty,' Billy replied calmly. 'It was my place to sign that contract, not yours. Don't forget that I'm your elder brother. And I ain't honouring no contract that I didn't sign.'

The hubbub started up again. Now there was an air of jubilation in the hall. Wilbur Hawkins glanced across at his lawyer and adviser but Tomkinson knew that they were beaten and he didn't even dare meet the banker's gaze.

Later that day stones were thrown through the windows of the Tomkinsons' house by drunken homesteaders who'd been celebrating their success in Roy Cole's Mexican Trail saloon. Worse was to follow: in the middle of the night the townsfolk were awakened by the glow of flames rising from Shad Jones' church hall.

The inhabitants of Cedar Hollow rushed from their beds and attempted to extinguish the flames with water drawn from the town's wells. Hixon and the other gunslingers watched them at work from an upper window in the Blue Star saloon. They made no attempt to leave the building, since they could guess what was going through the townsfolk's minds as they toiled in vain against the flames. Besides, Hixon knew that Wilbur Hawkins would be calling on them soon to start settling old scores.

FIFTEEN

Mary Liddell didn't sleep all night. Apart from the chaos caused by the fire in the church hall she was troubled by what Wilbur Hawkins had told her about the meeting of shareholders which had dealt a death blow to much of his vision for the township.

'The last person I expected to turn up at the church hall was your friend Billy Nash,' the banker told her over supper in his Blue Star saloon. 'I expected him to be well away from Cedar Hollow by now; he only got off that murder charge by the skin of his teeth.'

Mary said nothing but she felt terribly guilty that she'd kept mum about Billy's presence on the family homestead.

'The one I feel sorriest for is his brother Ty,' the banker went on sanctimoniously. 'Ty was left with

126

the responsibility for his dying parents after his eldest brother was killed in the war, and now that gambler fellow turns up years later and claims that everything belongs to him. Besides that, Billy Nash seems to have stirred the homesteaders up against me and Jeffrey Tomkinson so that now they've rejected our offer to finance them and help them improve their properties.'

By the time she got back to the boarding-house after supper Mary was harbouring her own ill-feelings towards Billy Nash. She'd gone out on a limb to save his stupid neck yet now he was deliberately thwarting and riling the man she was going to marry.

The next morning, as soon as she heard the full extent of the damage to the church hall, she visited the Jones family to commiserate with them and to offer any help she could.

'Thank you, Mary,' Emma Jones said as she ushered her into the living-room where her husband and daughter were sifting through the books and papers that had managed to survive the fire. 'People have been in and out all morning, including that so-called deputy marshal Ty Nash, though I sent him away with his tail between his legs.'

In the ensuing conversation it was apparent

that the pastor's family blamed Hixon and his gang for the fire the night before. In deference to their visitor, Wilbur Hawkins' name was not mentioned once, but she was left in no doubt as to their feelings.

At the end of her visit, Mary was accompanied to the door by the preacher's daughter Janie.

'I was even harsher to Ty than Ma was,' Janie informed her. 'I told him he was no longer a man, just Clem Nelmes' puppy dog.'

'Why Marshal Nelmes?' Mary asked. 'Nobody's mentioned his name.'

Janie snorted contemptuously.

'They're all in it together, Mary,' she said. 'Wilbur Hawkins, Jeffrey Tomkinson, the marshal, Hixon . . . Between them they control Cedar Hollow and they're going to do as they please with the town. Nobody is organized enough to stand up to them. I suppose my father is strong enough, but he's a man of peace – worse luck!'

Mary was still turning Janie's words over in her mind when she got back to the boarding-house. She felt sad that there was no common ground between the various factions in town. She knew that Wilbur only wanted the best for Cedar Hollow. If only he could explain himself better.

Miss Nellie Duke was waiting for her when she got back.

'You have a visitor,' she informed the young singer. 'She's waiting for you in the parlour. I think it's important, so I'll see that you're not disturbed.'

Mary Liddell went into the parlour and found herself face to face with a stranger, a handsome woman in her late thirties.

'I'm Kathryn Tomkinson,' the visitor informed her. 'My husband Jeffrey is more or less a partner of Wilbur Hawkins.'

'I .. I'm pleased to meet you,' Mary said, wondering to what she owed the honour of the visit.

'I've come to ask you to convey a message to Billy Nash,' Kathryn explained. 'It's very important. I assume that you're still in touch with him.'

By now Mary Liddell felt quite bewildered, and the mention of Billy's name didn't exactly fill her with enthusiasm.

'Why should I convey a message to Billy?' she said defensively. 'He's no longer a friend of mine.'

'They're going to kill him,' Kathryn said bluntly. 'Your fiancé and my husband are going to kill him. They plan to send Hixon and his men to the Nash homestead to gun him down. They

129

discussed it at our place last night, after the crowd had smashed our windows. Jeffrey and I are the most hated people in Cedar Hollow, Mary; and I guess we deserve it.'

Mary felt suddenly angry.

'What right have you to come in here and accuse Wilbur?' she demanded. 'What has he done to you?'

'Wilbur is my lover,' Kathryn told her. 'He's even slept with me since you arrived in town.'

'So that's it,' Mary said, her eyes flashing. 'You're mad with jealousy because you're losing him to me.'

The lawyer's wife smiled ruefully.

'Maybe you're right,' she agreed. 'I've lost him and I don't want him to have you. That's why I'm telling you the truth about him. I don't want you to love him. I don't want him to hold you up to me as a trophy!'

Mary saw tears forming in her visitor's eyes. They added a sense of urgency to her message.

'Whatever you think of me,' Kathryn Tomkinson went on. 'Whatever you think of Wilbur, I'm telling you what's going to happen. Unless you do something about it, Billy Nash is a dead man.'

SIXTEEN

Kathryn Tomkinson's visit had stirred up conflicting emotions in Mary Liddell. On the one hand she was betrothed to Wilbur Hawkins whom she considered to be an honest businessman with the town's best interests at heart; on the other hand there were the innuendoes she had heard the pastor's family utter concerning the banker's ruthless ambition. Then there was Billy Nash: she knew Billy to be a true friend, but what had made him oppose Wilbur – a sense of justice or merely sour grapes because of the forthcoming marriage?

She decided to talk to her fiancé and sound him out. That was only fair, she thought. She'd already repaid her debt to Billy Nash by saving him from the hangman's rope. It would be wrong of her to go behind Wilbur's back on the say-so of the jilted Kathryn Tomkinson.

She hurried along the main street to the bank, only to find that Hixon and his gang had beaten her to it. They were filing in one by one and they were looking very purposeful. That made up her mind for her. If the banker was about to give orders to these men, she had no time to lose. She passed the bank and made for the livery-stable.

Billy Nash was indoors when he heard the horse galloping down the track leading to the homestead. He went outside and his heart skipped a beat as he recognized the girl from her long blonde hair. However, he could only guess that she was here to rebuke him for his opposition to Wilbur Hawkins, so he looked just as serious as she did when she dismounted and they stood face to face.

'You've got to get out of here,' Mary told him breathlessly. 'According to Kathryn Tomkinson, Hixon and the rest of them are coming here to kill you. If she's right, you haven't got much time.'

Billy turned her words over in his mind. It made sense that they should want him dead; that might validate the company they'd set up, since his brother Ty would inevitably inherit the farm in the event of Billy's death. Mary Liddell took a deep breath before she spoke again.

'Listen, Billy,' she said urgently. 'When I left town Hixon and his gang were on their way into Wilbur's office. If Kathryn is saying the truth . . .'

Her voice trailed off as she realized the enormity of what she was saying – that her future husband was going to order the execution of a human being just because that human being stood in the way of his ambition.

Billy Nash could sense her dilemma and distress.

'Thank you Mary,' he said awkwardly. 'I really appreciate what you've done. Now you get on back to Cedar Hollow where you'll be safe.'

'What will you do?' she asked. 'Where will you go?'

He smiled philosophically and shrugged his shoulders.

'Nowhere,' he said. 'I'll wait for them here. It's as good a place as any.'

The next moment she was in his arms, pleading with him to flee. She turned her face up to his and he saw that she was crying. He kissed the tears from her cheeks and then their lips met and lingered before he gently pushed her away.

'Please go, Mary,' he told her. 'They won't want no witnesses.'

'If you're staying, then so am I,' she said defiantly. 'Just tell me what I can do to help.'

Marshal Clem Nelmes stormed into the Mexican Trail saloon and hurled a question at the owner, Roy Coles.

'You seen Ty Nash today?'

Coles didn't like the marshal enough to waste words on him, so he merely nodded his head in the direction of the table where Nelmes' deputy was slumped over a near-empty bottle of whiskey.

'Ty, you goddam useless sonofabitch!' the town marshal yelled at him. 'Get your ass off that chair. You and me got work to do.'

Nash raised his head and stared at him through an alcoholic mist.

'What's wrong, Clem?' he whined. 'I was just taking a little drink.'

The burly marshal strode over and hoisted him to his feet. The movement rocked the table and sent the whiskey bottle crashing to the floor.

'We're going visiting your brother,' he informed the drunk with a sarcastic laugh. 'You'd better sober up, else he's gonna be disappointed in you.'

The horses were already saddled up and waiting outside the saloon. Ty mounted his with difficulty. As they rode out of town he was still struggling to understand what was going on.

'Why are you taking me out to Billy's place, Clem?' he asked. 'You want me to give him another hiding?'

Nelmes gave him a look of withering contempt.

'Don't you see that Billy let you beat him, Ty?' he said. 'Maybe he thought it would give you some pride back. Nope, you don't have to do nothing – just be there. Hixon and his men have gone on ahead; they're gonna run your brother off the farm. Then it'll revert to you, and the homesteaders won't have a leg to stand on legally.'

Ty Nash was trying desperately to think clearly. What Nelmes was saying coincided uncomfortably with the tongue-lashing he'd got from Janie Jones that morning.

'But that ain't right, Clem,' he protested. 'They got no right to drive Billy off the farm. It's our home.'

'Your home?' Nelmes sneered. 'You don't own nothing, Ty. You're just like me. We do what Wilbur Hawkins tells us, that's all. If Hixon guns Billy down, you'll keep your mouth shut, understand?'

He failed to notice the strange expression on his deputy's face. The next moment the town marshal was desperately trying to keep his balance as Ty threw himself sideways and grabbed him around the shoulders. Startled, the horses drew apart and the two riders toppled heavily to the ground.

Both men fought and struggled as they rolled with the momentum of the fall, Nelmes to escape from his assailant and Ty Nash to attempt to squeeze the life out of the lawman. Then Nelmes managed to free his right hand and grope for the butt of his revolver.

The gun exploded with a muffled thud and Ty felt a searing pain in his right arm. He rose to his feet and saw that the marshal was still on all fours and winded. Then Nelmes levelled the Colt again and fired, missing his target by a hair's breadth. In desperation Ty lashed out violently with his right foot. The toe of his boot caught Nelmes square under the chin and his head shot back with a loud crack. The marshal slumped forward on to the brown earth, his neck splayed out at a bizarre angle.

'Clem . . . Clem!'

A cold sweat broke out on Ty's face as he knelt down beside Nelmes' body. The marshal's eyes were open wide, but they would never see again.

SEVENTEEN

A thick copse of deciduous trees stood a couple of hundred yards from the homestead and extended a good way up the slopes towards the north. For years it had provided the Nash family with firewood and building materials. Now Billy hoped to use it for self-preservation, since it was here that he intended to stand up to his enemies. A few days previously he'd felled an old oak-tree on the edge of the wood, and as he waited for them to show he busied himself with trimming the branches prior to sawing the hefty trunk into logs.

From time to time he glanced back at the house; all the windows were securely boarded up, and the only opening left was a tiny attic window. Mary Liddell had insisted that he let her station herself at that window with a loaded rifle in her hands. She assured him that she'd learned to use

a rifle while still a child, when she and her
parents had made up a family act in a circus back
East. Nevertheless, Billy had warned her to fire
only in an emergency, and then in the air so as not
to put his own life at risk.

'If they're out for trouble I'll hide in the woods,'
he told her. 'I know my way there and they're not
likely to follow me. With you safe in the house
they'll know there's a risk they'll be caught
between two fires. They won't like the odds and I'm
hoping they'll ride off again and think things over.'

She didn't ask him how long he thought it
would be till they came back again. She could only
pray that someone would find out what was
happening and would send help.

A cloud of dust on one of the hillsides betrayed
the riders' approach. Billy laid the axe down; he
knew he was going to be outnumbered, but at
least his visitors no longer had the element of
surprise on their side. As they drew closer Hixon
saw that the house was all boarded up, and his
first conjecture was that the homesteader had
decamped. For a moment he felt cheated of his
prey, but his disappointment was short-lived.

'That's Nash over there by the trees,' Davidge
announced with a broad grin. 'The fool's out in the
open.'

They rode up casually to where Billy stood waiting for them. Walsh noticed that the homesteader was wearing his gun, but he didn't reckon that he'd dare draw it, not with the odds at three against one. Walsh was badly wrong on that score and he paid for it when he decided to take the lead. Billy Nash knew why the three gunslingers had come and he knew that no amount of talking was going to deter them from their goal.

Billy let Walsh get within ten yards of where he was standing, then he drew his Colt in one smooth, swift movement and shot the gunslinger just below the heart. Walsh groaned and slumped forward in the saddle, while behind him Hixon and Davidge reached hurriedly for their .45s and struggled to get a good view of their assailant. Billy fired again and cursed himself for not taking more time over the shot since it missed Davidge by a mile. By now slugs were coming back in his direction so he wisely sought cover among the nearest clump of trees.

The horses were wheeling about in panic, so that Mary Liddell, crouched at the attic window, knew that it was unwise to risk a shot and betray her position. Much as she wanted to help Billy she realized the importance of keeping her presence hidden until she had a real chance of hitting something.

As she hesitated, the two gunslingers had dismounted and brought their horses under control. Hixon could hear the undergrowth cracking as Billy beat a hasty retreat into the woodland.

'You take cover here,' he told Davidge. 'I'm going after him. If he tries to make a break for the house, you can gun him down in the open.'

Davidge nodded; he was quite content to wait for more favourable circumstances to even their score with the homesteader. Hixon slipped silently amongst the trees. Everything was quite still now. Either Nash had got out of earshot, or he'd found a hiding-place. Hixon was an experienced gunfighter; he moved slowly and cautiously, listening and watching for any sign of life. Broken foliage told him that his prey had passed this way.

Suddenly he reached the edge of a small clearing. He halted and waited, hardly breathing. The minutes ticked by, but Hixon wasn't going to be fooled; if Nash was going to pick him off, this was the ideal spot for it. Overhead a crow circled and cawed irritably and drew a response from its partner some distance away.

A sudden crack caused Hixon's head to swivel

round. A bough had snapped some twenty feet above the ground and he saw Billy Nash slithering downwards through the foliage. Hixon jerked his gun up and fired but a loose branch swung across and took the full weight of the slug.

By now Billy Nash had realized that a fall was preferable to being shot so he stopped groping for support and concentrated on returning Hixon's fire. He landed awkwardly on his left side, but still thumbed the hammer of the Colt with his right hand.

Hixon stood looking down at him as Billy used up the last of his six shots. Then the gunslinger sagged against the nearest tree-trunk. Billy knew his life depended on how badly hurt his opponent was. With deep relief he saw Hixon sink slowly to his knees, blood oozing from his lips and his eyes glazed in death.

Ty Nash was close to the homestead when he heard the firing and reined his mount in the direction of the woods. When he reached them Davidge detached himself from the shadows to tell him what was going on.

'Hixon's gone after your brother,' he said. 'He told me to wait here.'

Ty's face was flushed and his eyes were feverish.

'You've got to stop them, Davidge,' he yelled. 'Goddammit, you gotta stop them!'

From her vantage point in the attic Mary Liddell got a bead on the newcomer as he reined in his horse. She felt nothing but bitterness towards Ty Nash, who must have come to support Hixon and the others. Even so, the tin star on the deputy's shirt made her pause for thought; he was a lawman after all, a bad lawman maybe, but still a lawman. It could mean big trouble for her and Billy if she shot him, even if he deserved it.

Davidge was also out in the open, so she turned the sight of the rifle on to him. Simultaneously Davidge drew his .45 and levelled it at Ty Nash's belly-button. Mary pressed the trigger.

Billy Nash could tell that the latest shot had come from the direction of the house. Mary must be in danger, he thought. Forgetting his own safety he ran headlong out of the woodland. When he saw his brother standing by Davidge's body he raised his Colt to cover him.

'One move and you're dead, Ty,' he warned him solemnly.

Ty turned to face him and Billy saw that his right arm was drenched with blood. Ty was wild-eyed and the words gushed out of him.

'I've killed Clem Nelmes, Billy,' he said.

142

'Hawkins sent us out here to gun you down, but I couldn't do it, and I couldn't talk Clem out of it. You've gotta help me, Billy. You gotta straighten things out.'

Ann Forest waited impatiently for the bank clerks to clear their desks and stash the day's takings in the solid iron safe. Soon she would be enjoying the best part of her day – working alone with her beloved employer Wilbur Hawkins, overseeing the figures produced by the cashiers. As the handful of employees filed out, she noticed lawyer Jeffrey Tomkinson lurking in the doorway, clutching a leather case to his bosom.

'I need to see Wilbur; it's important,' he told her tersely, then pushed past her and strode towards the door of Hawkins' private office.

'I don't think . . .' Miss Forest protested, but the lawyer was already turning the handle and opening the door.

'Jeffrey, what's wrong?' Hawkins enquired as his partner burst into the room. Normally he would have shown displeasure at such lack of etiquette, but this evening he was worried because he'd had no word from Hixon or Nelmes since he'd despatched them on a relatively simple mission to the Nash homestead. Maybe

Tomkinson had heard something.

The lawyer sat down in the chair facing him; he seemed tense and had developed a tic under his eye. He laid his leather case on the table in front of him and unclasped it. He slipped his hand inside it and let it rest there.

'Kathryn's told me everything, Wilbur,' he said, his voice full of bitterness.

'Kathryn?' The banker raised his eyebrows. This was an added complication that he could do without.

'Yes, she's walked out on me, but before she went she told me about your affair. I trusted you, Wilbur, just like I trusted Kathryn. Every deal I did with you, every petty, dirty trick was for her benefit, to keep her in the style her beauty demanded. And all the time she was cheating on me – you both were.'

At this moment Hawkins had more important things on his mind than the lawyer's hurt feelings.

'Anything that went on between me and Kathryn is long dead, Jeffrey,' he said. 'My future lies with Mary Liddell.'

'But I don't have a future, Wilbur,' Tomkinson replied pathetically. 'You've seen to that.'

He drew a revolver out of the leather case and

pointed it at the banker's chest. Hawkins noted that his partner's hand was shaking badly, so he made a lunge for the gun. As Tomkinson recoiled the revolver exploded suddenly and smashed a hole through the centre of the banker's face.

When Ann Forest rushed into the room, Wilbur Hawkins was sunk in his leather chair, his face a bloody mess. Jeffrey Tomkinson was slumped forward on the desk; he was sobbing uncontrollably. A scream froze in the secretary's throat as the enormity of the crime sank in. Then hatred took over and made her think more clearly.

She walked around the desk, opened a drawer and took out a single-shot derringer she knew Wilbur kept there. Without compunction she placed the muzzle of the small firearm against the side of the lawyer's temple and fired. Tomkinson's body suffered a brief, violent convulsion and then lay quite still.

There were replacement shells in the drawer. Ann Forest picked one of them up and calmly reloaded the derringer. She took one last, loving look at the disfigured face of her employer, then she turned the gun on herself and pulled the trigger.

EIGHTEEN

A week later Billy Nash was riding casually in the direction of Cedar Hollow when he spotted a lone horseman galloping along the trail towards him. When the rider got closer he turned out to be Pastor Shad Jones, and the foam around his horse's mouth indicated that the preacher was in quite a hurry.

'This is a stroke of luck,' he informed the homesteader. 'I was on my way to pay you a visit.'

'You could have saved yourself the journey, Pastor,' Billy replied. 'I'm on my way to town. I'm planning to ask Mary Liddell if she'll marry me. If the answer's yes, I guess we'll be needing you.'

The news didn't have the expected impact on the preacher, who still looked deadly serious. Billy began to feel uneasy.

'What's wrong?' he inquired. 'Is Mary OK?'

'Yeah, she's fine,' Jones answered, wiping the sweat from his brow.

'It's Ty, then,' Billy went on. 'Is he drinking again?'

The pastor shook his head emphatically.

'Ty hasn't touched liquor since he killed Nelmes,' he said. 'He calls in on us every day; and as for him and Janie, well, it's just like the old days again.'

'What is it, then?' Billy demanded. 'What are you holding back?'

'Yesterday a feller calling himself Josh Barlow rode into town,' the preacher replied. 'He says he's the last surviving Barlow since you shot his cousin in the back in Oakhill, Louisiana. He's challenging you to meet him on the main street in Cedar Hollow at noon today.'

Billy glanced up at the sun. It would be noon in less than an hour.

'Why didn't you let me know earlier?' he asked. 'What if we hadn't met up like this?'

'I wanted to let you know last night,' Shad Jones said. 'But Ty wouldn't hear of it. He says he's town marshal now that Clem Nelmes is dead, so he reckons it's up to him to deal with Josh Barlow.'

'But only a few days ago Ty's shooting arm was in a sling,' Billy protested.

147

'That's right, it still is,' the preacher agreed. 'But try telling Ty that – try telling you Nashes anything!'

'I've got to get into town pronto,' Billy said. 'Your horse needs a rest, so you won't mind if I go on ahead, Pastor. I cain't let no brother of mine get himself killed for my sake.'

When Billy Nash strode into Cedar Hollow's small jailhouse he found that Ty had another visitor – Mary Liddell. She turned to face the newcomer and he could see that her face was pale with worry.

'Billy,' she said. 'You shouldn't have come. There's been enough killing. Anyway, this is all my fault; if I hadn't sung in Oakhill none of this would have happened.'

She ran into his arms and he could feel her body shaking. He looked past her at his brother.

'How much time do I have Ty?' he enquired.

'Less than twenty minutes,' Ty answered, 'but you've still got time to get out, you and Mary here. Barlow's a wanted killer; it's my duty as a lawman to arrest him.'

Thoughts and memories of their childhood rushed into Billy's mind: brothers till death. Yet here was Ty urging him to run away from a bully

148

and a killer. Mary looked up into his face; it was set hard as stone. She wanted to tell him that Ty was only trying to help, but before she could speak his features softened and he even smiled.

'We're Nashes, Ty,' he said. 'You and me both. You know I'd never run away.'

'Sure,' Ty agreed. 'But last I heard Josh Barlow had a brother called Dill who specializes in bush-whacking. Josh reckons he's the only Barlow left but we cain't be sure of that.'

'Billy,' Mary Liddell said suddenly. 'There's been a stranger staying at Miss Nellie Duke's boarding-house for a couple of days. He eats in his own room and when he does go out, it's always after dark.'

Billy turned to his younger brother.

'I'm relying on you to check him out, Ty,' he said. 'Only don't take no risks. Take that badge off for a start; it makes you a target for fellers like the Barlows.'

Ty pulled himself up to his full height and looked Billy straight in the eye.

'I'm going out there as a Nash, Billy,' he announced, 'but also as Marshal of Cedar Hollow.'

He went out and closed the door behind him. Billy drew Mary Liddell against his body and kissed her fiercely.

149

'We don't have much time, Mary,' he told her. 'But there are things I've gotta say to you while I still can.'

Cedar Hollow had bounced back with surprising resilience and ingenuity after the death of Wilbur Hawkins and Jeffrey Tomkinson. The near-moribund town council had convened hastily with a new sense of urgency and purpose and had worked out an emergency plan to keep the bank open under the managership of the senior clerk. For his part, Pastor Shad Jones had contacted an old friend in a legal partnership in Fort Worth and soon an aspiring young lawyer would be arriving in Cedar Hollow to sort out the intricacies of the town's situation.

This morning, however, there prevailed a feeling of the calm before the storm. Folk had been urged to stay indoors because of the threat of violence, and most had heeded the advice. As Ty Nash walked along the main street he glanced over at the only empty building in sight. It boasted two storeys and many of its windows were boarded up, though glass still survived in one or two of them. The owner had died a year or two previously at an extremely advanced age, and his son who had long since moved to Arizona showed no inclination to come back and claim the property.

The building was the ideal hiding-place for a sharp-shooter, but Ty Nash knew that he had to call at the boarding-house to check on Mary Liddell's story. If the stranger she'd mentioned turned out to be Dill Barlow, it could mean serious trouble.

He was within sight of Miss Nellie's place when he saw the front door open and a slightly built man walked out into the sunshine. His Stetson was pulled down low on his forehead, so that his face was shaded and barely visible. He was carrying a newspaper in one hand, and he made straight for the Mexican Trail saloon along the street.

Now that Ty Nash had him under surveillance the lawman was in no hurry to intercept his quarry. He watched as the man sat down at a roughly hewn table in front of the saloon, spread the newspaper out wide and began to read. The time was ten minutes to noon.

Ty stood there for a while, waiting for the feller to make his move, but the stranger just sat there without even moving his head. Ty could see that the newspaper was just a bluff; the man's mind was obviously on other things. He decided to move in.

'Hey, mister . . .'

The stranger raised his head and stared at the tin badge on the lawman's chest. His eyes were sharp and taut.

'Sit down, Marshal,' he said, more as a command than an invitation.

As he spoke his left hand shifted the newspaper a few inches and Ty saw that his right hand was holding a gun, and that the muzzle was pointed directly at the lawman's stomach.

Billy Nash left the jailhouse a couple of minutes before noon. He'd warned Mary Liddell to keep well away from the windows in case of stray shots. At the far end of the main street a horseman was coming into view. It had to be Josh Barlow. Billy walked in measured strides to meet him.

He didn't even glance at his brother as he passed in front of the Mexican Trail saloon. The outlaw had dismounted and tethered his gelding near the bank. Then Barlow took up position in the middle of the road and waited for Billy to come to him.

Billy was glad that he had Ty at his back. Even

if Ty didn't get involved – and Billy hoped he wouldn't have to – it was comforting to know he was there. He got to within fifteen yards of Josh Barlow before the gunslinger spoke.

'You gunned down my cousin Cab, Nash,' he said accusingly. 'You didn't give him a chance.'

'He had every chance,' Billy corrected him. 'He tried to dry-gulch me. It was self-defence.'

The hairs rose on the back of his neck as he realized that Barlow's gaze was fixed on a point somewhere behind him. So Josh wasn't alone after all. He heard the sound of breaking glass and shots rang out. Then Josh Barlow went for his gun.

A safe distance away Emma Jones stood watching from the front steps of the small church. A few minutes earlier she'd been on her knees praying for good to prevail over evil. In fact, it was faith which decided the outcome of the duel, but not the religious faith which Emma and her husband embraced.

Both Billy Nash and Josh Barlow knew that they were dependent on their brothers for survival. For his part, Billy was confident that Ty would lay down his life for him. Josh, on the other hand, suspected that Dill Barlow's heart wasn't in the fight, since he'd tried to dissuade his elder brother from going anywhere near Cedar Hollow to avenge their cousin Cab's death.

Consequently, when Billy and Josh went for their guns the latter was over-anxious and his swift draw was marred by the slightest of fumbles as the Colt cleared the holster. Billy got the first shot in and smashed a slug into Barlow's shoulder. Confident that Ty would guard his back, he finished the job with a second slug that doubled the outlaw up and sent him tumbling in agony to the ground.

It was only when he was certain that Josh Barlow was out of the fight that he spun round to engage the enemy behind him. A hundred yards back a man in a Stetson was racing towards the empty building, emptying his six-shooter at one of the upstairs windows. Meanwhile, Ty Nash was running along in the stranger's wake, vainly trying to keep up with him, but hampered by the sling on his right arm.

The firing was not all one way; shots were coming from the window as well, raising small clouds of dust as they furrowed the ground.

'I'm going round the back, Slim,' Ty Nash called out as they reached the building. 'You cover the front.'

Inside the house Dill Barlow threw his rifle to one side. It would only hamper him in his attempt to get away. He risked his neck by racing down the rickety staircase. His horse was waiting in the alleyway and he threw his shoulder into the door to let himself out. He'd drawn his six-gun in readiness but he had no chance to use it.

'Drop the gun, Dill.'

Ty Nash was pointing his Colt .45 at the pit of his stomach. Dill realized that the game was up, so he let his gun drop to the floor. To his astonishment, the lawman sheathed his Colt and smiled apologetically.

'I cain't use it,' Ty said. 'I ain't never shot a man.'

The gunslinger couldn't believe his luck. There was less than a yard between them. He made a grab for the marshal's revolver and walked straight into one of the best left hooks Ty Nash had ever thrown.

When Billy Nash arrived on the scene his brother Ty and the feller in the Stetson were looking down at the outlaw who was stretched out cold.

Billy stared at the stranger.

'You're Slim Forbes, marshal of Oakhill,' he said.

'I *was* marshal of Oakhill,' Forbes corrected him. 'Dill and Josh Barlow gunned down my nephew Hank. The townsfolk were too chicken to form a posse so I threw in my badge. I've been trailing these men ever since and it was made easier for me because I knew they were trailing you. You've killed Josh Barlow for me, but I won't rest till I see Dill Barlow hang.'

As he spoke Ty Nash was looking very pensive. Suddenly he unpinned the tin star from his shirt and handed it to Slim Forbes.

'Well, this should help you, Marshal,' he said. 'I'm quitting and going back to farming.'

Forbes gazed at the badge and a slow smile formed on his lips. Over the past couple of days he'd grown quite partial to Miss Nellie Duke's cooking, indeed to Miss Nellie Duke herself.

Meanwhile Ty had turned to his elder brother.

'D'you reckon there's room for both of us on the homestead, Billy?' he asked. 'Like in the old days?'

Billy Nash glanced back in the direction of the jailhouse. Mary Liddell was standing on the front step, her blonde hair dancing in the sunlight.

'I'm going away, Ty,' he said. 'I'm going away with Mary.'

He could see the disappointment on his

brother's face and it made him feel warm. He was home at last.

'Don't worry, Ty,' he smiled. 'We won't be gone long. Just a honeymoon . . .'

T. MIX.